THE DRAGON'S AMBIVALENT SACRIFICE

THE LAST DRAGONS BOOK 2

INES JOHNSON

THOSE JOHNSON GIRLS

Copyright © 2019, Ines Johnson. All rights reserved.
This novel is a work of fiction. All characters, places, and incidents described in this publication are used fictitiously, or are entirely fictional. No part of this publication may be reproduced or transmitted, in any form or by any means, except by an authorized retailer, or with written permission of the author.

Edited by Alyssa Breck
Cover design by Jacqueline Sweet Designs

Manufactured in the United States of America
First Edition October 2019

CHAPTER ONE

*S*nap. *Crackle. Pop.*

The crown of Beryl's head crashed back, nearly touching the space between his shoulder blades. His Adam's apple stretched the inside of his neck as though it would break the skin there. The force of his head flinging back caused his upper lip to catch his incisors. A grunt tore from his throat.

The sound wasn't one of pain. He licked the blood of his split lip. A smile curled at his mouth, making the cut spread wider and the pain sting more.

He swaggered back to his opponent. The beast of a man was the same height as Beryl and just as broad. Leander's barreled chest was covered in a blond mat of fuzz that curled as salty beads of sweat trickled down into the tendrils. His massive paws were nearly the size of Beryl's head. The weapons ended in claws.

That was fine. Beryl had claws of his own, and they were just as sharp. Golden fur met green scales as lion and dragon clashed in the ring.

Beryl shoved the lion shifter into the corner. He had him on the ropes. The gathered crowd cheered. Beryl turned, raising his hands into the air to accept the praise.

Berylmania was ripe in the crowd tonight. If he had a yellow shirt on, he'd tear it from his chest. But yellow wasn't his true color. Up in the crowd, there were a few emerald green bandanas with the golden letters of his name written across. The fae pumped their fists in the air and shouted his name and his title.

Beryl, the Heavyweight Champion of the Veil.

In his corner, his brother Ilia shouted instructions like, "Go for his knee," or "Don't turn your back," or "Pay attention, and don't get cocky." All of which Beryl didn't listen to. He was the champion, not Ilia who hadn't won his match earlier against a wolf shifter.

From behind, Beryl felt a slash at his shoulder

blades. And then a blow was delivered to his side. He doubled over and received a swift kick to his face.

He saw red, then stars, then black.

Blinking his eyes rapidly, Beryl scrambled to his feet. There were two Ilia's shaking his head in the corner. There were two Leanders coming at him from the opposite corner. Blinking again, the two lions merged into one fierce predator intent on his prey.

Silly cub. Didn't he know? Dragons were at the top of the food chain in this land beyond the Veil. And Beryl was the biggest, baddest, fiercest dragon of his clan. The best fighter in all the Veil. It said so on his flashy title belt.

Not taking his eyes off his opponent this time, Beryl crouched. Digging down on his haunches, he waited for the attack. He wasn't known for his patience or his cunning, just his brute force. When it came to fighting, strategy simply came naturally to his big blockhead.

When Leander was just two steps away, Beryl unfolded his wings from his back and launched himself into the air. The lion's perfectly curled hair lifted, getting mussed as Beryl's powerful wings carried him over the male and to his back. Beryl gave one swift kick to Leander's sacrum. The lion roared as he went to his knees. With lizard fast speed, Beryl grabbed Leander around his neck and put him in a submission hold. Apex predators did not like to be cowed. Survival of the fittest was a moniker that began with shifters, not mankind.

The fairies, trolls, and other shifters gathered in the bowels of God's Teet roared their approval. Up in a special section, sat the Valkyrie. Dragons might be at the top of the food chain, but the Valkyries had that chain wrapped around their manicured fists. The leather-clad women were the keepers of the peace of this ragtag bunch of unnaturals. Unnatural because all the beings in this realm were engineered and not evolved like the plants and animals in the human world.

Once again, with Beryl's attention diverted, Leander got out of the hold. The lion tucked his chin and rolled into the crook of Beryl's elbow as they'd seen Hulk Hogan do with Andre the Giant. Beryl knew Leander's favorite wrestler of all time was the massive giant. They'd both spent enough time in Beryl's man cave watching the Wrestlemania III match. But didn't the lion know how that match ended? If not, he was about to get a fresh reminder.

"Now, we face each other as God intended;

sportsmanlike. No tricks. No weapons. Skill against skill alone."

Beryl rolled his eyes as Leander quoted his favorite film. The giant of a lion's paw struck out, catching Beryl in the eye. Beryl's dragon was elated. The beast couldn't wait to see the new marks. It liked the blood, it needed the violence. It was the only thing that soothed his inner beast. Not the only thing that could. Just the only means available to him.

Beryl fought his brothers on a daily basis. It was required for their dragons who day by day were becoming more beasts than men. Fighting kept them in some semblance of balance. But the scales were tilted against them. And not just the dragons. The balance was out of whack for all male shifters in the realm.

Beryl was done playing with the lion. He danced around his frenemy, light on his toes, moving his feet quickly. He was always pretty when he fought. He liked to put on a show for all watching.

The female fairies in the audience sighed audibly over the crunch of bone and mashing of flesh. The air was permeated with their honeyed scent of arousal. Looking up, Beryl saw the fae gazing at him. The flower creatures were all easily bendable with their vine-like limbs. He could have his pick of flowers tonight, but his gaze kept slipping to the Valkyrie. The bloodthirsty huntresses were more interested in their ale than the fight. Valkyries bowed to no one. But they did have one weakness.

"You done flirting?" said Leander. "Or should I leave the ring so you can go toe to toe with those flowers?"

"You've got other things to worry about, brother," said Beryl. "Whatcha gonna do when Berylmania comes for you?"

Leander rolled his eyes and charged. He leaped into the air on two feet as a man and landed on four as a massive lion. Powerful paws drummed into the floor of the ring, making the whole place shudder with his ferocity. He opened his mouth, incisors dripping, and roared. The air around stirred like the beginnings of a storm.

The dragon had been pushing against Beryl's skin all night. Finally, Beryl let the beast have his body. It was the only way he would have satisfaction tonight. Besides, it wasn't as though he could control his shifts much anymore. If the dragon wanted to get out, it would.

Beryl's claws scraped against the floor as he landed. The two beasts clashed at the center of the ring. Leander got in a few more good jabs until Beryl got his claws around Leander's body. He lifted the massive lion into the air and body-slammed him just as his hero Hulk Hogan had done to Andre the Giant in their final match.

The impact shook the establishment. A wave of beings bounced out of their seats and then jumped to their feet, roaring their approval. With Leander on his back, Beryl was able to get him into another submission hold. This hold stuck because, unlike the man who could be easily distracted, the dragon had a singular focus.

Pain.

Inflicting pain was the only thing that brought the beast to heel. And so he tightened the screws around Leander's mane.

The lion's head was too big. He couldn't tuck his chin and duck out this time. Leander's only option was to tap out. After long moments trapped in the dragon's clutches, Beryl felt Leander's claws tapping on his arm.

He'd done it. He'd protected his title. The fight was over. So why was Ilia still shouting instructions from the corner?

Beryl ignored his brother and reveled in his victory. Many of the male shifters had been fighting in these cage matches for weeks now. Not one had bested Beryl. Not the bears or the wolves. Not his brother. And now, the mighty Leander, King of the Beasts, had fallen.

Beryl looked down at Leander. His lips were blue. His eyes were bugging out of their sockets.

Oh, crap. He still had him in a chokehold. He needed to let go. Only, his dragon didn't relent.

Beryl tried to loosen the beast's hold, but the dragon was too powerful. It wanted the lion's blood.

Beryl looked into the lion's eyes as the life was slowly seeping out of them. There was recognition there. This was Leander. His friend. They play fought when the two of them were just fledglings. They shared a love of weightlifting and working out, seeing who could grow their muscles the biggest.

Leander's muscles were straining now as the breath left his body. The lion hadn't even wanted this fight. Beryl had goaded him into it the only way he knew how. Leander had a secret, one he'd only told Beryl. And Beryl had threatened to reveal it to the whole realm if Leander didn't join him in the ring.

Inside himself, Beryl was fighting a losing war. His dragon tasted blood in the air, and it wanted more. Was this it? Was this his last moment as a man as the dragon took complete control over his body like his brother Rhoyl's had done?

Maybe so because somehow, Beryl was flying through the air without ever remembering launching.

Beryl's wings unfurled and caught the current before he landed. His dragon turned, ready to face the next foe. And stopped right in its tracks.

A blonde woman, smaller than the lion but with a fierce glare, squared off before him. She stood over the unconscious lion shifter. Though she was the official of the match, her round face and strong cheekbones belied her connection to the limp male on the mat.

Instantly, Beryl's beast gave way to man. He stood at the center of the ring stark naked, his beast having ripped his clothes off in the change. Beryl bowed his head in shame, not meeting the woman's gaze.

"My apologies, lioness."

"Control your beast," growled Leona, "or you won't be invited over for playtime with my boys anymore."

"Yes, ma'am."

The matches had been Leona's idea. She had been the one to approach Beryl. He hadn't questioned why the mother of six male lions had organized the matches. It had been obvious; she was the mother of six male lions. She needed some way to get their aggression out that wouldn't add more damage to her den.

Leona turned to her son. She didn't check his wounds or even help him up like a normal mother would. Because she was a lioness. When she saw that her eldest was still breathing, she turned back to the crowd and announced Beryl the winner.

The crowd chanted his name. With his past fights, this had been the highlight of the match, hearing cheers for what felt natural to him. But with this match, he felt like he'd lost the contest.

He had lost something. He'd lost himself. He had no grip on his animal. If Leona hadn't intervened, Beryl wasn't sure he'd have regained control. He could've killed Leander. And Beryl actually liked the big, hairy, pretty boy. Better than he liked his own brother.

"That was bad sportsmanship," said Ilia as Beryl climbed out of the ring. "You should've gone for his knees instead—"

"Shut it." Beryl gave his brother a shove.

Ilia, who was a foot shorter and a stone lighter than Beryl, fell back into a throng of fairies. The flowers caught him in their veiny clutches. Ilia's brown eyes flashed jade, his dragon surfacing in response to Beryl's assault.

Beryl felt a twinge of remorse, but he quickly tamped it down. Ilia was used to this treatment being born the runt of the litter. And Beryl didn't have time to apologize. He had more important things to attend to.

He made his way through the cheering crowd. Not bothering to cover his manhood as he did.

"Let me heal those wounds," said a fae. Dahlia was her name.

He'd had her several times. Her sweet scent usually called to him, but it was bitter tonight. He hadn't indulged in fairies for a while now, not since he knew there was a chance.

Beryl side stepped Dahlia and made his way to the Valkyries who were leaving.

"Siggy? Hilda? Any news back from beyond the Veil?"

Hilda turned to him, braids whipping as she turned. Her sword raised and arced at his throat. Beryl swallowed. Her blade caught the bob of his Adam's apple.

"What do I look like?" Hilda's lip curled as she regarded him. "The Nightly News?"

Beryl held up his hands in a placating fashion.

"My apologies. I was only asking if you've had any word from Morrigan?"

"Morri isn't back from her hunt," said Siggy. Her gaze was unabashedly on Beryl's package.

A few weeks ago, Beryl's brother Corun had made a deal with the Valkyries to bring back female sacrifices for them in exchange for gems. Beryl had pulled Morrigan aside and offered her her weight in emeralds if she brought him the first catch. But he hadn't seen hide nor hair of the Valkyrie since then.

"I'll double the fee if you join her hunt." Beryl let the dragon rise to the surface. His eyes glowed emerald green.

The Valkyrie's gazes flashed golden with desire. This was the fierce warriors' only weakness. They loved gems. They loved most things sparkly. Dragons mined gems and were notoriously covetous of their treasures. But dragons treasured having a sacrifice more than the gems in their mountain.

"We don't work for you," said Hilda, but the bite had gone out of her tone. "We are not here to manifest your private booty call."

It wasn't a booty call. It was a lifesaver. A sacrifice, a woman of his own to protect, provide for, and pleasure was the only thing that would permanently soothe his beast and keep it on a leash.

If Beryl didn't get a sacrifice soon, his dragon would take over the body they shared, and the man would be trapped inside. Otherwise, he'd have to continue to fight in these cage matches to keep a semblance of control. If tonight proved anything it showed, that with his control waining, in the next fight someone might die.

CHAPTER TWO

"Are you tired of your humdrum everyday existence?"

Poppy Maddow looked up from the ironing board. On the square television screen, a blonde woman with a perky smile raised one of her eyebrows in a conspiratorial gaze. The woman peered at Poppy in standard definition from the twelve-inch screen, but Poppy felt she saw straight into her heart's desire.

"We live on a beautiful planet filled with stunning landscapes, breathtaking views, and tropical paradises."

Poppy glanced out the window of the single-wide trailer. There wasn't much to see. Except for barren trees, rusted cars up on blocks, overflowing trash heaps, and a garbage dump that had once been a muddy pond.

"Then come with me and escape into a world of picturesque mountains, emerald waters, and medieval towns."

On the twelve-inch screen, the camera displayed a flyover of green waters but not like the sewage green of her backyard. She could see into the depths of the waters on television. Unlike the barren forest outback, lush green leaves topped each tree. The brown covering the landscape on the show was sand and not the dirt and grime of poverty.

Poppy leaned forward, eyes wide, heart thudding, feet aching to run away to this marvel.

"Where the fuck are my pants?"

Poppy didn't jump at the gruff bellow. She'd been yelled at all her life. Bruce's raised voice was normal for her.

She opened her mouth to let him know that she was ironing the pants he was looking for. Instead, she choked, no words escaped her mouth. Looking down, she saw that there was a dark spot on the right pant leg. While she'd been entranced with the exotic getaway, she'd forgotten about the iron, and it had scorched a spot on Bruce's best pants.

Shit. She was in for it.

Poppy scrambled to hide the evidence. Unfortunately, there wasn't much space in the trailer. Every room did double duty. The kitchen was also the dining area. Each cupboard was filled to the max with glass pots, pans, tubes, and other tools and utensils to make the soul-stealing drug that kept this tin roof over their heads. So, she couldn't stuff the pants there.

The only option was to stuff the pants up her sundress. That was one place Bruce wouldn't look. He might spread her thighs in the middle of the day if he hadn't gotten any from one of his tricks during the night, but he would never look at her while he was doing it.

"Did you hear me, you ugly bitch?" Bruce said, rounding the corner out of the bedroom which doubled as a living room. He was in dingy, tight briefs with his beer belly spilling over. His hairy chest was bare. There was a hole in the toe of his blue socks. But it was his dress socks. Clearly, he had somewhere important to be, and he needed those jeans, his best outfit.

Double shit.

"Did you check the laundry basket?" Poppy asked innocently. She patted her stomach, trying to look natural and not like she was carrying a baby.

One thing she did not skimp on in her impoverished state was birth control. She was at the neighborhood clinic every month like clockwork for her pills. She did not want to bring a baby into this miserable life that she wanted to get out of herself.

"You were supposed to be doing the laundry." Bruce stormed up to her. His footfalls shook the trailer on its foundation. "I can't put your ugly ass on the street to earn. You're allergic to the fucking chemicals that make my product. What the fuck use are you if you can't keep my house, bitch?"

He shoved her, but there wasn't really any place for her to go in the cramped space. Her back hit the stove, and she slid down its surface. The pants slipped out of her dress.

"What the fuck?" He snatched his pants before she could hide them again. Before she could offer an apology or get out of his way, the back of his hand met the side of her face. "Fucking useless cunt. These are real Gucci knockoffs. I paid fifty bucks for these."

A couple of months ago, she'd burned the steak he'd stolen from a restaurant kitchen. That had been twenty-five dollars-worth of meat. He'd struck her once for that. Fifty bucks was a fortune. Poppy raised her arms, waiting for a second strike.

"Cover yourself up," Bruce barked.

He tugged down her dress, but the worn fabric didn't stretch far enough to cover the ugliness on her legs. He turned away from her. The spots on her limbs were one of the reasons he didn't look at her when he did her in the middle of the day.

"You know what I should do?" he said, still crouched over her. "I should put your ass in a glory hole. No one would have to see your ugly ass then."

His breath was heavy with the stench of another woman's cunt. His nails were dark with the grime of his nighttime job as the local pimp of the trailer park. The veins in his biceps were scarred from the abuse of his product.

Poppy pulled her knees up to cover the tender spots on her legs. The discoloration made her bare skin look like a leper's. That's what they used to call her in grade school when the spots had started to appear. The doctors all said she didn't have the disease. They were at a loss as to what was wrong with her.

Her mother had had the same skin condition. It hadn't stopped her from working the streets. That was one of the only job choices here in the backwoods of Knudsen. Either work on your knees cleaning or work on your back tricking.

Kellyanne had been determined that her little girl would never be on her back. But Poppy had ended up on both ends of the short stick. She began her days on her knees, cleaning Bruce's pigsty and doing laundry for his tricks who worked the streets. Then she lay on her side at night hoping he wouldn't come home and turn her on her back.

It wasn't a bad life. Other girls had it far worse. She got to spend most of her days alone as the other women gathered at the edge of the trailer park waiting for drivebys. She'd salvaged the TV which got public television, including travel shows like *Globe Trekker* where she got to see the world. And there was even a channel that ran old dramas like *Knight Rider, The Incredible Hulk*, and *Beauty and the Beast* but in Spanish.

No, it wasn't a bad life at all. Sure, she got hit from time to time. Sometimes she even deserved it. Like now. She had been careless and ruined Bruce's best pair of pants.

"I think I can fix this," she said through the sting in her jaw. "I just need a little vinegar. Let me try."

He scowled at her for another full minute before backing up. He didn't offer her a hand. She scrambled to her feet, making sure to keep her spots hidden from his sight so as not to antagonize him any further.

Poppy scavenged through the cabinets looking for the vinegar. She found the bottle just as the next load of laundry dinged. She tended to Bruce's pants first, dabbing the acid into the burn mark. Thank goodness, it looked as though it was coming out. Maybe she wouldn't get that second slap after all. The day was already looking up.

She sat the pants aside to dry and went to tend to the laundry. Poppy pulled out a mix of thongs and short skirts that could double as bandanas. Her hand froze on one set of undergarments.

The garment wasn't a woman's size. The tag indicated size by ages. It was a child's. Ages six to twelve. The white cotton displayed hugging teddy bears. In the crotch were muted streaks of blood.

Poppy's dress strap slipped off her shoulder as she rose. She didn't pull the strap back up to cover the spots on her arms. More than anything, she wanted to rip the dress off her body. The thin cotton suddenly felt like sandpaper on her tender, disease-riddled skin.

"What's taking you so long? I gotta get out there. Are you as stupid as you are ugly?"

She wasn't sure how the butcher knife came to

be in her palm. When Bruce's hand came down to clasp her shoulder, she turned and slashed out at him.

Bruce's gaze went wide with shock. His hand clutched at his cheek. Blood dripped between his fingers.

"You said you'd never touch a child." Poppy's voice was small as it fought its way out of her chest. She held the knife in one hand and the child's underwear in the other.

Bruce's eyes cleared and filled with rage. "That little whore begged me for work. She wanted it. And now you're going to get it."

He advanced on her. Poppy slashed the knife again. But Bruce was far more practiced in giving violence than her. He got hold of her hand, stripping the knife from her. All she was left with for armor was the ruined panties of someone's baby girl.

It was only the second time in her life that she'd considered fighting back. The first time, she'd been wearing size-age-eight panties with unicorns and rainbows. They'd been ripped from her small body, but before any blood could be let, her guardian angel had come to her rescue.

Poppy teared up like she always did when she thought of her mom. Kellyanne was long dead now.

There was no one coming to rescue her. Not from this life. Death couldn't be worse. At least she'd get out of this trailer park and see something else outside her window.

She turned her head toward the window, preparing to take Bruce's fist. Wait? Had he already struck her? Or was there something in the window?

It was not only a new view, but it was also a new person. The woman sitting on the ledge had on far too many clothes to be considered a prostitute. The corset she wore would be a prized garment for a streetwalker. The boots too. But no one in this trailer park could afford or would bother with tight-fitting leather pants that would take precious minutes to get on before a John could get off. And they'd have to be dry-cleaned. No, whoever this woman was, she was not here for tricks.

The well-dressed woman cleared her throat just as Bruce raised the knife for his strike. From the corner of her eye, Poppy saw Bruce turn to the window. His mouth gaped when he saw what was there.

"I would say pick on someone your own size …" The woman's eyes dipped to Bruce's manhood in his tighty-whiteys and held. "But that would be unfair of me."

"Who the fuck are you?" Bruce pointed the knife at her, no longer concerned with Poppy's imminent demise. Why would he be? She wasn't going anywhere anytime soon.

"I ..." The woman hopped down from the window, the impact of her boots shook the trailer more than Bruce's steps. "... am your ride."

An uncertain smirk began at the corner of Bruce's lips. "Oh, yeah? Where we going, baby?"

The woman pulled a long glistening sword from her back. The blade was more than five times as long as the knife in Bruce's hand. "Straight past Hell to somewhere far, far worse. And lucky you, it looks like you're dressed perfectly for the occasion."

Bruce opened his mouth for a retort. A gurgling sound came out of his throat because she had sliced a gaping hole across his neck. Blood poured out where words were meant to go. Bruce's body fell to the ground with a sickening thunk.

Poppy stood frozen. Her body was too afraid to even shake with fear. When she looked over, the woman was eying her. Not her face, her hand.

The woman lifted her hand, the one without the sword, and made a come hither motion to Poppy. Her fear of violence had trained her well. Without hesitation, Poppy did as she was told. Her steps were slow and stiff, but she crossed the short distance to stand in front of the woman.

The woman reached out and took the child's panties from Poppy's hand. "This one's been on my radar for a minute, but this latest act was his death knell."

She used the panties to wipe Bruce's blood from her blade, covering the hugging teddy bears with the essence of his expired life. It seemed fitting. His death for innocence lost.

"Looks like it was your last straw, too." The woman's eyes glowed bright, like stars, as they swung from the discarded butcher knife and back to Poppy.

The only answer Poppy could give was to gulp. She'd had a counselor stop by the trailer once, dressed in a buttoned-up dress and shiny shoes. Bruce had knocked Poppy a good one the night before. The counselor's gaze stayed trained on that spot. When Poppy refused to leave with the counselor, she asked why she stayed. Poppy let the creaking screen door slam in the woman's face.

She'd seen a few of the movie dramatizations of wives escaping husbands in the dead of night with flawless eye makeup and glossed lips. She'd even seen enough daytime talk shows about domestic abuse where the well-meaning host offered up cash services and a back door to escape. None of that was the real world.

Seeing Bruce lying dead on the floor, Poppy didn't feel any remorse for him. But she did begin to worry about herself. She had no schooling, no skills. She didn't even have a pretty face. How was she going to support herself now?

Poppy ran a hand through her hair. Her fingers were shaking as she did so. The woman's gaze narrowed as they followed her movements. Lightning fast, she reached out and tugged down the top of Poppy's dress.

Poppy gasped. Reflex told her to cover herself. Self-preservation balled her grasping fingers into still fists.

"Red hair and scales? Is it my lucky day or what?"

Poppy squirmed to get out of her hold. A wicked grin had spread over the woman's face. Poppy knew that look. It was the look of a predator.

"You're going to fetch me a pretty gem."

Poppy turned to run. But she felt a thud at the back of her neck. And then everything went black.

CHAPTER THREE

The clanging of metal meeting metal resounded through the underground cave. Beryl had heard that human men had man caves inside their houses; a small room where they could retreat away from women. He didn't understand why a man would want to retreat from his woman. If he had a woman, he would let her inside his cave any time she wanted. He would build her one of her own and sit inside the doorway hoping he'd be welcomed into her inner sanctuary.

He had an actual cave inside the castle he shared with his brothers. Many of the rooms were caves outside of the actual caves where the brothers each mined their gems and hoarded their treasure.

Except for Corun who had given his treasure

away for his female sacrifice. Beryl would've done the same. His new sister was worth every gem, and soon Chryssie would add to their family. Two whelps were growing strong inside her belly.

There was a downside to Corun and Chryssie's coupling. The two were one of the reasons Beryl was currently in his mancave. They were going at it like rabbits on a constant basis.

"If you can go through this pain period, you may get to be a champion," said a thickly accented male voice. "If you can't go through it, forget it."

Beryl turned down the volume of the film on the television. It was the only thing he agreed with that came out of the Austrian's mouth. He fast-forwarded the VHS tape past the parts with Arnold Schwarzenegger to see his hero Lou Ferrigno. Ferrigno was robbed of the Mr. Olympia title in the film. He was so much better, so much bigger than the Austrian.

Aside from fighting, pumping iron was the only other thing that soothed Beryl's beast. Once Beryl could content himself with boinking fairies. But the wilty women held no interest for him any longer. He wanted a flesh and blood woman. One he could call his own. One his dragon could sink its teeth into and claim.

It had been weeks since Morrigan had agreed to find him a sacrifice. He wasn't sure how much longer he could hold on.

"Did you take my Terminator speedos?"

The weights clanked again as Beryl let them fall to the floor. Over him stood a male with glowing, dark eyes. As always, the runt of their litter was ready to pick a fight to assert his dominance.

"Why would I touch your underwear, Ilia?" Beryl shrugged, grabbing a Classic Coke from the refrigeration unit that Morrigan had brought back some time ago. "They would never fit what I'm carrying."

Ilia scoffed. "You may have got the height amongst the three of us, but I most certainly got the girth."

Beryl knew he shouldn't give in to the petty argument. Like him, Ilia was just itching for a reason to throw his fists. Neither dragon had anything better to do.

Beryl had already benched a thousand pounds. His blood was still pumping and overworked after his fight yesterday. It might soothe him to pound his brother in the face for a few minutes. The only problem was, he wasn't sure he had his beast wrangled enough to not actually kill Ilia.

"You're just mad Arnold won the title," Ilia sing-songed. "You know the Terminator would beat the Hulk any day."

And there snapped his control. Beryl rose. It didn't take much for the dragons to fight. Those were serious fighting words. Everyone knew the Hulk was stronger than that hunk of mealy-mouthed metal.

Beryl nearly shifted as he faced off with his brother, but he held himself back. He was wearing a Gold's Gym T-shirt. The Valkyrie said that particular garment was getting harder and harder to find beyond the Veil. He didn't want to ruin this one. It was his favorite.

"Whatever," said Beryl. "If you want to root for the bad guy who travels back in time to destroy all of humanity, then go have at it. The Hulk fights for the underdog."

"Does not," was Ilia's retort. "Bannon can't control the beast inside of him. But the Terminator is all control."

"Oh, yeah? If the Terminator is such a hero, then why does he die in a burning vat of fire never to return?"

Ilia had no retort for that. The Hulk might be out of control, but he was always on the side of good. And the Terminator only got one film, and he died at the end. Bannon kept working to keep the beast under control. They hadn't seen the end of the series, but Beryl was certain the green man and the human had to come to harmony one day. They were heroes. That's what heroes did.

Beryl stormed passed his brother. But his beast continued to pace inside his gut. Maybe he should go find a fairy to relieve some of this pressure in his lions. Who knew when Morrigan would return with his sacrifice. And even if she did, he'd likely have to fight his other brothers for her.

Well, only Ilia. Elek had no desire for a mate. Rhoyl couldn't do anything with a mate if he tried, being that he'd been stuck in dragon form for years.

So, it would just be him and Ilia. Ilia looked for any reason to fight. The runt of their litter was always aiming to prove himself in the family of bigger males.

Beryl caught sight of Elek as the silent man walked in and out of the shadows of the castle. He was likely headed to visit his mother. Miyaoaxochitl had been nonresponsive since she'd delivered Elek and lost his brother.

Corun and Chryssie were in their rooms above. Kimber was in the mines. His mate Cardi, who wasn't yet of age to claim, was likely in the game room playing a videogame; one of the fighting ones where she got to use a weapon to explode men's heads off their bodies.

Beryl thought he saw Rhoyl flying out the window. But, no, it wasn't his brother's blue scales. This dragon had brown scales. Only purebreds had brown scales.

Beryl recognized the dragon. It belonged to the Valkyrie, Morrigan. She was here.

With Ilia down in the man cave, Beryl could get to the sacrifice first. He could mark her, and she would be his without a fight. He raced to the back door just in time for the Valkyrie to land.

"Where is she?" Beryl demanded.

"Slow your roll, scaly boy." Morrigan hopped from the dragon's back. "I've got a lot of things to unload."

"You have her? You have my sacrifice?"

"I have Cardi's John Hughes collection of angsty redheaded girls who chase after boys. Or wait? Is it just one girl? The same one every time? I can't tell. All humans look alike. I have Corun's ultrasound machine so he can spy on his whelps, which tells you what kind of parent he will be. And you were looking for the newest *Donkey Kong*—"

"Enough," Beryl growled.

The Valkyrie's eyes glowed dangerously bright.

Beryl dipped his head. Dragons might be at the top of the food chain in the Veil. He could roar at his brothers. He could choke out a lion. But he wouldn't survive a Valkyrie's wrath or sword. The daughters of the Goddess were beyond the food chain.

Up above, Beryl saw Rhoyl's blue scales shimmer in the moonlight. His brother hovered, watching them. From a window, he saw Elek looking down, amber eyes glowing in the night. Rhoyl and Elek would join the fight if it were necessary. And they'd both perish.

"Please," Beryl said. He was a desperate man. He was barely holding on to his beast as it was. It was aiming to rip the Valkyrie's head off, something that would spell certain doom for man and beast.

Morrigan sauntered around her dragon. There were two human-sized sacks on its back. Beryl smelled blood coming from one. That had to be her capture for Valhalla. The Valkyrie usually didn't kill their prey before bringing them beyond the Veil. Briefly, Beryl wondered what had caused such ire for her to kill the man early.

But that sad sack was instantly forgotten in favor of the second. Beryl's gaze flitted to the sack the Valkyrie removed. Morrigan lifted it with no effort.

Beryl could smell the delectable scent coming off of it. It smelled of something sweet but not from nature. There was also an acidic smell that reminded him of the potions in Corun's lab. Underneath all of that was the smell of something light, like a breeze over a small body of water. He reached for the sack.

Morrigan snatched it back. "Unh unh unh. Payment first."

Beryl grit his teeth. "Follow me."

He led the Valkyrie into the entrance to the mines. He skirted past Corun's ruby mines and Kimber's diamond mines. He took the entrance into his own mines where emeralds were buried beneath the rock.

"Take what you want," he said to the Valkyrie.

Her eyes glowed again but out of greed instead of anger. She handed him the sack and went shopping.

For a moment, Beryl just held the sack in his arms. She weighed nothing, but she felt heavy with importance. Slowly, he pulled back the sheath of fabric to reveal a round face. Soft strawberry curls framed her face. A small button nose split her features into two perfectly symmetrical halves. Her lips were small, heart-shaped, and full.

"There's fire in her blood?" Beryl asked.

Like it mattered. The bundle in his arms was his,

and he was keeping her whether she could birth him whelps or not. If she had no fire and couldn't carry a dragon, he could still hold her and protect her. His beast didn't need the physical to sate him. He just needed a cause. And she was his cause.

"She's a fire blood."

Relief sailed through Beryl. The words he'd thought a moment ago crumbled in his mind. She was beautiful, and he wanted her physically. With the confirmation, his loins ached to have her this very instant.

"Even better," said Morrigan, "look closer, she has scales."

Cradling his prize in his arms, Beryl slipped the cloth from her delicate shoulders. He gasped at what he saw. On her pale skin were golden spots. They were soft to the touch, but he knew instantly what they were.

"What's her name?" he asked.

"I didn't ask. Gird your loins, though. She was about to castrate my mark before I could claim him."

Beryl grinned at that pronouncement. His female was feisty, just like Cardi and Chryssie. She was perfect. He uncovered the rest of her and began the ritual of binding.

CHAPTER FOUR

She was definitely dead.

How did she know for sure? She was being snuggled. Snuggling only happened with moms in the real world, and her mom was dead.

Since she was young, Poppy had seen many a mommy backhand a kid, or strong-arm them in the direction they wanted them to go, or give them a shove or a pinch to get in line. But Poppy had lucked out. Her mom gave her snuggles in bed from time to time. But only during the times her mom's bed wasn't occupied with a client.

Those were the times Poppy felt safe. Those were the times she didn't have a desire to fly away to some imaginary world she'd seen on television.

When she was inside her mother's arms, the

world stopped being a dangerous place where food was scarce, and voices were always raised, and men looked at little girls like afternoon snacks.

It had been an afternoon when Poppy had lain in her mother's bed and dozed. School had let out early, and she'd come back to an empty trailer. When arms came around her, they hadn't felt warm. They'd been sweaty and rancid with the stench of unwashed man.

No.

Poppy's eyes were closed in the present. She shut them tighter. She wouldn't go there. She was safe, dead, and finally back in her mother's arms.

Her mother had taken care of the stinky man who'd put his dirty hands down Poppy's clean underwear. There had been blood on the bed, but it wasn't Poppy's. And then her mother had brought Poppy into her warm embrace.

It was the last one she'd ever had.

Until now.

Poppy had known death was nothing to fear. Now, she could be back with her mom. She'd get warm hugs for all eternity.

It was just, had her mother's hugs always been so tight? She'd used to be able to twist her body and turn to lay her head against her mother's beating heart. She couldn't do that now.

Her mom's arms had always been thin. Just not as thin as a piece of rope. Also, her mom had two arms, and they weren't that long. But somehow they were wrapped around her arms, her stomach, and her legs.

Something was wrong. Poppy lowered her head to quiet the rising nausea. Her chin was able to touch her chest, but her stomach clenched. She opened her eyes and saw that she was indeed in an embrace. Ropes cradled her, not her mother's pale, track-marked, man-bruised arms.

For a moment, she could only stare and admire the handiwork of the ropes. They crisscrossed her body in an intricate pattern. She looked like she'd been wrapped like a gift. She waited for the fear to claw at her, for the need to escape to drown her.

It didn't come. She couldn't help the sense of peace that washed over her at being bound. She felt secure, safe.

Great. So, she'd lost her mind in death as well as her freedom.

It was still better than being in that shithole with Bruce. It couldn't be too much worse, being the slave to that angel of death. At least Poppy wouldn't have to lie on her back to earn her keep.

Or so she hoped. Were angels lesbians? Did they have sex? They must do it to make angel babies.

She'd considered lesbianism in her teens after her first sexual experience with a boy. Later she rejected it when Joanna Wilcox, the homecoming queen, and meanest girl to walk the hall, came out of the closet. What was the point of switching teams if brutes existed in every sexuality?

Sex or no sex, there was an even worse issue with her new captivity. Her spots were showing. The ropes rode the dress up on her thighs. Being bound was one thing. Bruce had tied her up before. He'd even locked her in a closet once for getting the wrong brand of beer. But being on display like this would not do.

Poppy squirmed. She moved her hips right and left, trying to get the hem of her dress into her hands. If she could just give it a tug, she could cover the biggest spot on her right thigh.

"Stop," said a deep voice. "You'll hurt yourself."

Poppy did as she was told. Partly because of the command in the man's tone; she had been broken into obedience from a young age. But mostly because the voice was that of a man. It looked like

she would be working on her back again after all.
And with a man who liked his victims helpless and
bound.

"I smell fear on you, little one."

Little one? If that was his idea of an insult, she'd
heard worse. Pimpled Prostitute, Trailer Park Tigger,
Dirty Dalmatian. She'd survived those, she could
live with Little One. But what did he mean by he
smelled fear?

"No one and nothing here would dare harm
you."

With the ropes pressing into her skin, Poppy
doubted that. But she knew better than to argue with
a man. It brought nothing but pain. Still, she was
exposed, and embarrassment pushed words from
her throat.

"Please, mister, I don't like to be exposed."

"Exposed?"

His voice sounded like it had been given to him
by a bear. It was way too deep to be that of a man.
Then he moved, and the room flooded with light.

Poppy had thought she was in darkness. Her eyes
had just needed time to adjust. When they did, she
went slack against the ropes. Her exposed spots went
forgotten.

She wasn't in a room. She was outside. Or rather

inside something that was outside. There was a scent of fresh earth in the air, along with that damp chill that came from being close to a body of water at night. There were rocks all around her. She had to be in a cave. The green gems sparkling from the rocks cinched that idea. She was in an emerald mine.

The man who'd spoken to her came into view. He towered over her, blocking out the green light. The green was now coming from his eyes like they were made of emeralds. His face was cruelly beautiful, sharp angles and chiseled bone. He was built like a wrestler, but he looked like a model; a fitness model for a bodybuilding magazine. His bulging muscles were stuffed into a yellow Gold's Gym T-shirt over gray gym shorts that left nothing to the imagination.

One meaty hand lifted to her face. Poppy braced herself for her first punishment. Instead, a warm hand brushed down the side of her face. The gentleness of it shook something inside her. Never had a man handled her with anything resembling care. Were things backward in death?

"Are you cold, little one?"

"I ..." She wasn't sure how to answer?

Poppy didn't understand the question. It had

nothing to do with him or his needs. It appeared to be centered on her. Was he asking about her wellbeing? About her comfort?

All other questions about herself had been along the lines of *Are you stupid?* Or *Did you get dropped on your head?* Or *Where's my dinner?*

The big man pulled his shirt over his head. Poppy was treated to the sight of muscle upon muscle. He dropped the shirt over her engulfing her in warmth and his scent. He was sweaty, but it was nowhere near approaching stench territory. He smelled of fresh air and warm heat and man. His shirt covered her from her shoulders down to her toes. With her spots under wraps, she relaxed and inhaled more of his scent.

"Tell me your name?" he asked as she tucked the edges of the shirt around her body as though it were a blanket.

"Poppy."

"Pop pee."

"It's Penelope. But everyone calls me Poppy."

He made a rumble in his throat and then said her name. Over and over again, like it was a chant. Poppy stared at his mouth as he formed her name.

"I am Beryl."

"Hi, Beryl."

"Hi, Poppy."

She grinned back at him. "Beryl, I'm sorry for asking, but is there a reason you've tied me up?"

"You've been bound for your protection," he said.

"My protection? From what?"

"From me."

All the warmth left her middle and flushed out her fingers and toes. "You're going to hurt me?"

"Never." He spoke so vehemently that she believed him.

"You have been given to me as a sacrifice," he said. "The rest of my life will be spent ensuring your comfort and pleasure."

Again his words made no sense. Sacrifice? The rest of her life? Her comfort and pleasure?

"You no longer have anything to worry about. I'll take care of everything for you."

Nope. Still not registering.

"But before that happens, I must mark you."

"Mark me?"

"This will hurt. But only for a second. Then I promise you nothing but pleasure for the rest of your days."

Her eyes were fixed on his lips and his teeth moving closer to her. She found herself arching her neck toward him. A second before he clamped down, a loud thud sounded behind him, and another man darkened the doorway.

"Stop," growled the newcomer. "I challenge you for her."

"She's mine!" roared Beryl.

There was a thunderous explosion as the green-eyed man and the dark figure clashed. Poppy's voice caught in her throat. Her bound body went tense. She could do nothing but stare at the violence unfolding before her.

eryl ducked Ilia's first punch. It was easy as his brother was as predictable as a robot. As slow as one too. That was the reason the Terminator lost to two, puny humans. When Beryl ducked his brother's punch he caught sight of her; his mate.

Poppy.

She was everything he could've ever wanted in a mate. She spoke softly, which pleased his beast. There was so much yelling and posturing in this castle. Even Cardi and Chryssie raised their voices and, though his beast loved the two, he shrank each time they shrieked.

But not his mate. Poppy had only struggled because she was cold. An oversight on his part.

Thank the Goddess he'd covered her before Ilia could see her body and the beautiful scales covering her flesh. Beryl's incisors had watered at the sight, eager for a taste.

Ilia's jab to his head caused Beryl to bite down on his lip. He tasted blood. It wasn't what he'd planned to have on his lips. But it helped clear his head.

"I challenge you for her," shouted Ilia.

The runt of the litter was always challenging one of them. He'd given up challenging Kimber and Corun as the two were now mated and settled. Rhoyl would only fight in dragon form. And Elek simply didn't care enough to assert any dominance. So that just left Beryl as the brunt of Ilia's mantrums as Cardi called them.

"She's already chosen me," said Beryl.

"You haven't marked her," said Ilia.

"'Cause you crashed a party where you were unwanted."

Ilia's scowl dropped, and anguish colored his features. He had been unwanted when he was born. Their father had left Ilia outside to die, believing he wasn't strong enough to survive. At times, Beryl believed the only reason Ilia did was to prove the beast of a man wrong.

Beryl hadn't meant to bring that sore spot up, but

he couldn't have Ilia crash his mating. He got in another jab and cross. Ilia tumbled back. His eyes flashed the dark jade of midnight. Scales pushed out of his flesh, claws extended from his fingers. He leaped up on legs and landed on thick dragon hindquarters. Fire flamed out of his mouth.

As a man, Ilia was slight. But his beast was a behemoth. Nearly twice the size of Beryl's. The dragon had protected the little boy who had been left to die and grew into a ferocious protector. But this was one prize Beryl was unwilling to give up. Ilia's dragon was also reckless, more reckless than Beryl's. The dragon did not like to lose and would go to extreme measures to win.

Beryl dashed in front of Poppy and spread his wings just in time. Heat bloomed to the top of the cave's walls down to Beryl's toes. He took it all, bearing the brunt of his brother's careless blaze.

"Stop," Beryl roared. "Or you'll hurt her."

That was the only thing that could ever calm a crazed dragon. The reality of putting a woman in danger. The flames immediately died down.

Ilia's dragon gasped, pulling the flames back inside of himself. He shifted back into his human form and rushed forward. "I'm sorry. I'm sorry."

Beryl shoved his brother's chest, pushing him

down to the ground. Ilia fell on his bare ass. He didn't put out his hands to catch himself. He didn't put them up to ward off Beryl's rough kick to the gut.

"You are not worthy of her," snarled Beryl. "You can't even control your beast."

He was one to talk. He'd nearly killed a man last night because his beast was out of control. But in this, he was right.

He was also in complete control of himself and his beast. Ilia wasn't. He couldn't have her. He'd nearly burned her to a crisp.

"You're far too reckless for a mate."

Ilia hung his head, much like Beryl had done after his fight where he'd nearly killed Leander. Ilia's shoulders hunched. Though he wasn't sporting a long dragon's tail any longer, his ass sank between his legs as he trudged off and out of the room.

Beryl turned back to his mate. Her eyes were wide with shock. He took her chin in hand. He turned her to face him. The moment her eyes connected with him, she screamed.

She hadn't made a peep the whole fight. The shock must have just worn off. Beryl winced at the shrill sound but waited until it was all out of her.

"Please, don't hurt me," she begged. "Please, I'll be good."

"I would never let a hair on your head be harmed."

Her eyes were still filled with fear. His dragon paced back and forth inside him. It didn't like the smell of her fear. It urged him to bury his face between her thighs. Pleasure would take away the fear. But Beryl wasn't the blockhead others believed him to be. He knew better. He knew that would only scare her more.

He brushed her tears away. She winced at the prick of his claws. A small trickle of red blood pooled at his claw tip. He cursed under his breath. He'd just broken his promise to not hurt her, but it was an accident.

He had to remind himself to be gentle. She was human. She was fragile. She was precious.

He retracted his claws. The room changed from bright green to normal colors as his dragon sat back on its haunches and let the man have total control.

Beryl set to work loosening the ropes binding her. When he was done, he pulled her into his arms. She didn't fight him. That helped to settle the beast inside him. She was covered in his scent. She would accept his mark; she would accept his claim.

In his embrace, she held still. Tension rolled off her small form in waves. "I don't want to be dead anymore," she whimpered, her eyes shut firmly closed.

"You are very much alive, little one."

"I want to wake up." She rocked her small frame inside his arms as though she were trying to soothe herself.

Beryl cradled her closer, rocking her gently. "You are awake, my precious gem."

"What's happening?" Her hands were balled into fists against his chest. He could feel her throat working, swallowing again and again as though she were trying to get something large and bitter down. "Am I going crazy, or did that man just turn into a dragon?"

Beryl nodded. Then realized she couldn't see him. "Yes."

"And you're a dragon, too?"

"I am."

The swallowing stopped. Her head tilted back, and she looked into his face. She was even more beautiful than she had been a moment ago. Small and warm and delicate.

His to protect.

"You said I'm your sacrifice," she said.

"You are," Beryl confirmed.

"Are you going to eat me?"

A wicked smile spread across his face.

Poppy's face contorted into misery. "Please, please don't. I'm a good worker. I'll clean for you. I can cook, not well, but I'll try. I can do your laundry, and I promise not to burn anything."

"My beautiful, little one. You won't have to lift a finger for the rest of your life. I'll take care of everything."

He brushed his lips across hers. Not in a proper kiss. Barely a taste. He just needed to know how she felt.

She was as soft as he imagined. The little gasp that escaped her mouth was so sweet. He could live off the taste of her flesh for the rest of his days and never go hungry.

His beast reared up. The dragon had been calm for a moment. But now that it had its first taste of its mate, it was rampaging to get out again.

Beryl had wanted to take his time with her. To smooth the rest of the fear in her eyes away. But neither man nor beast could wait for a second longer to take what was theirs.

"I'm going to mark you now so that none of my other brothers try to claim you."

He opened his mouth. The dragon roared as his incisors lengthened. Before he tasted her flesh, he tasted her fear. Her whimper filled his ears. The crease in her brow stretched in terror. But he could not stop himself.

He struck her shoulder with his teeth. Biting hard until he met bone, sinking his scent deep into her body until his essence pumped through her veins. The marking was a give and take. As he fed his soul into her, his heartbeat synched with hers. As much as he'd taken her as a mate, she'd taken him too. With one bite, Poppy became his entire world.

CHAPTER SIX

She was being bitten. A man with wings and green eyes was biting her. He wasn't a vampire; he was a dragon. But he might still be the devil.

That was the only explanation for what she'd just seen. Two demons fighting over who would get to eat her. She almost wished the other one had won. She didn't want Beryl, who had shown her a little kindness, to now rip that apart with his teeth.

Poppy opened her mouth to scream when his teeth sank into her. The sound died on her lips. It was replaced with a low moan of pleasure. His bite didn't hurt. It felt … almost orgasmic.

Not that she'd know. She'd never actually had one. Only seen it on porn sites when Bruce was up late at night, with the volume up so loud she couldn't sleep. But this felt like what she'd seen in glorious Technicolor on his laptop.

Her body was shaking, trembling. She felt her temperature rising in real-time. Like she was getting a fever. But she didn't feel weak or weary like when she had a cold or the flu.

She felt as though Beryl was infusing strength into her. She was floating through the air. But then she realized it was because he'd lifted her.

She sat on his lap in a gentle cradle of warmth. He was all muscle and brawn. But he handled her like she was a delicate piece of lingerie not meant for the regular cycle.

There were still scales at some points in his skin. Dark green like the emeralds all around her. Was she going crazy or did his spots look like hers?

Her fingertips brushed against them. But when she looked again, they were gone. All that was left were his muscles, and there were lots of them. She expected hardness, but he was soft to the touch.

And he'd stopped biting her. He licked her blood off his teeth and then sucked at his lips. The corners of his eyes crinkled, like she did when she bit the edges of chocolate chip cookies right out of the oven.

She'd never given a man pleasure. She'd never known how to. Never truly wanted to.

When Bruce would come to her bed smelling of the streets and cheap beer, he'd simply part her thighs, pump a couple of times, and rollover. She was a means to an end, and she was fine with that. Sex was currency in the world she'd come from.

The low grumbling coming from Beryl's throat awakened something in her. She wanted to taste nice for him. She wanted to be a delicacy on his tongue. She wanted to be enjoyed by someone at least once in her life, even if it was in death. Because she had enjoyed his bite.

Even now, her thighs were pressed together, seeking traction. Her nipples had pulled to tight points. They never did that unless she was cold. Certainly, no man had ever gotten a sexual reaction from her.

With his bite, Beryl had turned on a switch inside her. She wished he'd part her thighs and pump for a while. She wished he'd grab a handful of her breasts and squeeze some of that tension out of her nipples.

But he didn't. Instead, his green gaze bore down on her. He was searching her face for something.

"I'm sorry I hurt you. I swear it will never happen again."

"I'm not hurt," she said. "Well, it did hurt at first. But then it stopped."

His throat worked, as though he were trying to swallow a huge lump down. "I'm big, and you're small."

Way to state the obvious.

"But I swear, I won't hurt you."

She believed him. But she did have a question. "Am I going to turn into a dragon?"

She couldn't believe the hope that rose into her chest at that. If she turned into a dragon instead of his next meal, maybe he'd bite her again. Maybe he'd want to do more with her than sink his teeth into her. Or perhaps, he'd sink them elsewhere on her.

Beryl smiled at her. Her breath caught when he flashed twin dimples. His eyes were brown now, but there was a spark of green in his pupils.

"Of course not," he said. "You'll remain a woman."

Disappointment warred with relief. She wouldn't become a dragon, which was a bummer. But he'd also said she'd remain a woman. Well, that was good. Maybe he'd bite her again then.

He gazed down the length of her body with hunger. "You'll remain curvy and perfect."

Poppy shook her head, as though she could dislodge the misplaced compliment. "I'm not perfect."

Beryl's smile faded. His gaze narrowed on her in displeasure. "If you speak about yourself that way again, I'll be forced to punish you."

Here it came. Poppy didn't even flinch at his words. They were expected. The violence that followed her around all her life had finally shown up in this place.

What would it be? A backhand across the cheek? A hand around her throat? Or a new litany of insults from this silver-tongued dragon.

She wanted to cower, but there was no place for her to go. He still had a hold on her. A gentle hold, but one that she couldn't break out of inside his cage of muscles.

"You belong to me now. Do not speak of my treasure as though it were trash. I will not stand for it."

Poppy swallowed at the vehemence in this voice. Her brain could not comprehend his words. He was displeased with her for talking bad about herself?

What was she supposed to do? Pretend she was

worth something? The best thing would be to remain silent.

As he pulled the last of the ropes from her body, his T-shirt slipped off her shoulders, exposing her spots. Poppy reached to cover herself.

"Did I hurt you?" Beryl pulled her hand away. "Are you injured?"

"I ..."

"I was very careful with you."

He cradled her head in his hand. His gaze searched her face, roaming over her lips, then her cheeks. His eyes, which were now brown, flashed green when they met hers.

"Goddess, forgive me," he whispered, shame lacing his deep voice.

Beryl brushed his thumb beneath her eye. Poppy winced at his gentle touch. Her mind flashed back to the source of that pain.

"No, that wasn't you," she said, wrapping his thumb in her hand. The single finger was so big her hand barely closed around the single digit. "That was from ... the last man I belonged to."

Beryl grit his teeth, but his hands remained gentle. "I'll kill him."

For someone who hated violence, those harsh

words, spoken so gently, ignited something inside of her. "He's already dead."

Beryl took a deep breath and let it out slowly. He was visibly calming himself. In the quiet moment he took to collect himself, Poppy felt a peacefulness wash over her. It was a new sensation. She hadn't had a moment without fear, without stress, without anxiety in her whole life.

Beryl pulled his T-shirt off her body and shoved it over his head. Poppy didn't hide her disappointment that his muscles now had a second skin.

"Did he harm you anywhere else?" Beryl said.

"No." She knew the lie was easy to hear in that single syllable. But she didn't want to go through the long list of slaps and punches and kicks. Or the daily verbal abuse. Or the unwanted sexual interludes which she had to lay there and take in order to ensure her survival. A strong man like Beryl would never understand what she'd had to endure just to eat every day.

His gaze continued to survey her body, clearly not trusting her words. His eyes dipped once again to her spots, examining her skin there. The skin that was heavily discolored by her disease.

"Those aren't bruises," she said. "They're a disease. It's not contagious or anything."

Beryl brushed his fingers over the largest spot on her upper arm. "These aren't a disease. They're scales. You have fire in your blood."

"Scales? Fire?"

He nodded, brushing his fingertips across them with something that looked like reverence. "You have dragon's blood running through your veins. That's why you're perfect for me. My perfect mate. My treasure."

CHAPTER SEVEN

Cradling Poppy in his arms would be the highlight of his every day. He was surrounded by gems all day. He knew how to extract them from the clutching rocks without damaging their sparkle. Poppy was all sparkle.

Hair like flames that fell down her back in waves. He could see his mark on her shoulder, red against her pale skin. Far too pale for his liking. Did she not get enough sun where she came from?

No matter. She was never going back there. She'd stay in his arms for the rest of his days.

A squeak came from her lips.

"What is it?" Beryl clutched her to him, searching for the danger.

"Nothing."

Hearing the lie, he studied her face. He felt the anger roiling inside of him, burning him up as though his blood was toxic gamma radiation. He was going to Hulk out and lose control. But instead, his dragon whimpered at what it saw.

Poppy wore a wince on her beautiful face. She seemed to struggle for breath. She squirmed in his arms as though she were caught in a snare.

It was him. He was squeezing her too tight with his arms.

Beryl loosened his grip immediately. Catching her at the last second before she crashed to the ground. Her eyes were wide with alarm. She smelled like fear.

Beryl dropped to his knees. "Forgive me, my treasure. Sometimes, I don't know my own strength."

"It's okay. I'm fine."

More lies. Inside his gut, his dragon was rampaging again. Why didn't their female trust them? Likely because he kept inflicting harm at his every turn. Why couldn't he transform into Bannon for her; a normal-sized, gentle man who was smart. But then who would protect her if he morphed into the weak scientist instead of the towering Hulk.

Beryl stood, aiming to give her a wide berth. His dragon refused. He needed to have his hands on her.

"May I hold your hand?" he asked. "I promise I'll be gentle."

He gritted his teeth as she hesitated. Poppy looked at him as though she didn't believe his words. Finally, she exhaled. Wonder of wonders, a small smile crested one side of her mouth.

Beryl held out his hand. Poppy placed her small one in his. Her fingertips were rough, the skin ragged.

Had his precious gem been put to work in the human world? No longer. With him, she wouldn't have to lift a finger.

He closed her hand in his and guided her out of the caves. She stumbled down the steps, so he swept her into his arms. It was late at night. The moon was a full circle overhead. Beryl let his wings unfurl. Poppy gasped, her hands going immediately around his neck. The move pleased man and beast as his female sought him for protection.

He wanted to fly her around the entire property. But that would not be safe. Not during a full moon with an unclaimed human female. He'd have to fight every manner of shifter in the realm; lion, bear, wolf.

He landed at the back door to the castle. They slipped quietly inside. Dragons were nocturnal, but the three human women inside would be sleeping.

Beryl couldn't wait to introduce his mate to Cardi, Chryssie, and Miya. Though Miya would have no response, she was still the only mother figure to all of them, and Beryl wanted her to see the new treasure he'd unearthed. But for now, he would keep Poppy to himself, starting with his favorite place in the castle. His workout room.

Aside from the mines, this was the place Beryl spent most of his time. Lifting weights was more than a passion of his, it was a way of life. This room was where he sculpted his body into a finely honed machine.

He waited for Poppy's reaction, trying not to bounce on his toes with anticipation. Her gaze went around the room, taking it in. The weights had been left out and weren't on the rack. One poster peeled from the wall. He noticed the sweaty smell now. And in the corner, he spotted Ilia's speedo.

Why hadn't he cleaned before bringing her here? She'd surely think him a sloth.

"It's usually much tidier," he said.

"No, it's fine."

There was that phrase again. *It's fine.* He was coming to see that when she said those two words, she meant the opposite.

"I like *The Terminator*, too," Poppy said, indicating the poster curling off the wall.

Beryl's jaw clenched hard. His belly roiled at her statement. He waited, hoping she'd add the words it's fine to the statement. She didn't. His mate was a Schwarzenegger fan. What cruel joke was this?

Poppy pulled out of his grasp and started for the weights. "I can get to work on it straight away."

"Get to work?"

Beryl trailed behind her as she bent to the weights. She put her hands around one of the small twenty pound weights. He became distracted at seeing the curve of her ass that he didn't realize her intention until it was too late. Then he became distracted by the grunts she made as she tugged at the weights.

Beryl reached down and picked up the weight in one hand. "What are you doing?"

"This is what you brought me here for, right? To clean your house?" She bent down to collect the speedo.

"You will do no such thing." He caught her shoulders, pulling her to standing and away from Ilia's underwear.

Poppy's face contorted in pain with a tinge of

fear. Her gaze was wide as she stared directly into Beryl's eyes.

Directly into his eyes?

Beryl cursed. He was holding her in the air. Her feet dangled a few feet off the ground.

He sat her down gently. Her hands went to her shoulders to massage the hurt he'd placed there. He put his hands over hers to take over the job. She went stiff at his touch. The fear was still there, but the scent wasn't as strong.

"Poppy, I'm sorry."

"It's fine."

It wasn't fine. The tone of her voice confirmed it. "You are small and delicate. I am big and rough."

"I'm not so delicate," she said in her small voice.

"I'm supposed to provide for you, to protect you. How can I do that if my very touch brings you pain?"

"Are you sending me back?"

Her fear hit his nostrils at full blast. His dragon peeled back the layers and found the sweet scent of her. It wanted to pounce. Beryl wrangled the beast into submission. He needed to listen to his mate. He needed to understand that scent of fear.

"Back?" He frowned. "Back to your world? No, never."

The sweet fragrance of relief wafted off her body, but the bitterness of the fear was still there.

"Are you going to give me to that other dragon?"

"Ilia? No."

The remaining sourness was pushed to the edge of her fragrance. But still, it lingered. His dragon demanded that he get rid of the foul aftertaste.

"You're mine," Beryl said. "My life will be dedicated to your happiness."

She chewed at her bottom lip. There was the slightest crinkle in her brow, as though doubt weighed heavy on her mind. Why didn't she look convinced?

"What about the angel?" she said.

"Angel?"

"The woman with the sword who brought me here."

"You mean the Valkyrie." Chryssie had also thought Morrigan was the angel of death when she arrived. "What about her?"

"Isn't she your girlfriend?"

"Girlfriend?" Beryl knew the word. It was a human term. One he'd heard often in the movies and television shows Cardi watched. "She's a Valkyrie."

That didn't appear to register with Poppy.

"I don't think they even like men. She brought you to me in exchange for gems."

All worry and doubt fell from Poppy's brow. To be immediately replaced with shame. "So, I'm a whore."

"No!" He definitely knew that word from television. It was a slander thrown upon women who either sold their bodies for money or who slept with more men than was the cultural norm.

He saw how she could've gotten that idea with the transactional nature that began their relationship. But the gems were just the delivery service. He couldn't cross the Veil. Now that she was here, she would be worshipped. No other man would lay a hand on her.

"I see we have a new lady of the evening." Elek's soft voice carried from the corner of the room as he materialized from the shadows.

Poppy's back went rigid, her face blank. Fear no longer poured off her. Her fight or flight response was high, and the smell was overwhelmingly tinged with the desire to flee.

Instinctively, Beryl wrapped his arm around her waist. His huge palm spanned all of her back. His thumb reached the right side of her hip, his pinky finger rested on the other side.

She didn't cower from him. Her body canted toward him, as though seeking shelter. His beast purred inside his gut at the slight action.

"Poppy, this is my youngest brother. His name is Elek."

Elek inclined his head while keeping his distance. "Do you like sweet things in your mouth, Poppy?"

The pungent aroma of Poppy's horror punched Beryl in the nose. Elek smelled it as well because he lowered his head, making himself appear smaller. It was unnatural for a dragon, an apex predator, to perform such a move. But males would go out of their way to please females.

Poppy ducked behind Beryl's large body. The fact that she sought his protection made his beast preen like a fairy showing off its first blossom of the spring.

"I brought sweetmeats and greens." Elek presented a platter of food. He handed the platter to Beryl instead of coming close to Poppy.

Poppy leaned around Beryl's body but didn't go beyond his bicep. She eyed the food with suspicion. Her eyes darted from the food and back to Elek. "This is for me?"

Elek nodded, raising his head slightly to meet her gaze.

"You made me food?" she asked.

"I wasn't sure if you prefer sweet, savory, or salty. So there's some of each."

On the platter were three dishes; a savory meat dish, a vegetable dish whose salty spices that made Beryl's lips water, and a sweet dessert of flower blossoms. At the edge of the platter was an amber colored gem that looked like a tiger's eye. It was Elek's offering to his new sister.

When Beryl looked up to thank his brother for the dish and his acceptance of his mate, Elek was already gone. Disappeared into the shadows.

"I don't understand this place," said Poppy as she stared down at the platter of food Elek left. "I'm not here to clean or cook. You say I'm not a whore. Then what exactly is my purpose here?"

"To be adorned and adored by me."

The look of puzzlement on her face made him want to take her into his arms and kiss her senseless. It was only his dragon's desire to feed her that was stronger.

"Let me feed you while I explain."

CHAPTER EIGHT

Nothing made sense anymore.

Being bound felt freeing. Being bitten felt good. And men cooked?

She wasn't here to be a snack. She wasn't here to die. She was here to belong to this gentle giant who could give her pleasure with just the sharp points of his teeth.

Poppy followed Beryl up the stairs of the castle. Did she mention she was in a freaking castle? And she'd been inside an emerald mine. The last hour of her life had been the most adventurous, and they were just getting started.

If she hadn't believed him before, she knew it now. Beryl meant her no harm. Not only that, but he would fight for her. He'd proven that when his first brother had tried to take her. And then he'd shielded her when his second brother had—well, he'd only brought her food. But Beryl had sensed her fear, and he'd held her to him like a real live boyfriend would on TV.

He even opened the door for her. Of course, it led into a bedroom. It was clearly a man's bedroom. It was clearly Beryl's bedroom.

Right. Here was the part where the television would turn to static and real life would begin. Here was where Poppy would earn her keep.

He'd said he would provide for her, protect her, and pleasure her. He had already protected her from his brother. He still held the delicious-smelling food in his hands which would be provided to her. But now it was time to pay the bill by giving him pleasure.

She looked around her new workspace. It completed her still-forming opinion of the new man whom she would belong to. He was definitely a muscle head.

Which was a plus for her. It meant no one would bother her. And he was so gentle with her.

Aside from the ropes, which had made her feel safe.

And the bite, which had given her an almost-orgasm.

The door snicked shut behind her. Poppy's gaze stayed trained on the furniture in the bedroom. The bed frame was made out of gym equipment. The frame was metal. The headboard was made of rods and plates from Bowflex exercise machines. Poppy knew because she often stayed up late with insomnia and saw the infomercials featuring Chuck Norris and Christie Brinkley.

Despite the intimidating workout gear, the bed itself looked functional. Poppy had never worked out a day in her life. She'd always been skin and bones. Beryl had called her curvy, though she wasn't sure where he saw any roundness. Would he expect her to do reps while he pummeled her?

Her attention caught on something to the other side of the room. "You collect dolls?"

That was unexpected, but it eased some of her tension. On the dresser was an array of plastic men. Some in army fatigues. Others wore colorful costumes but had their ribbed abs exposed.

"They're not dolls," Beryl huffed. "They're action figures.

He picked up the Hulk doll—action figure—and raised its fist.

Looking closely, Poppy recognized some wrestling superstars. Not because she watched the WWE, but because she'd watched the *Hulk Hogan's Rocking Wrestling* cartoon show that came on one of the Spanish language public access channels in the trailer park. She'd always cringed from the violence, but she enjoyed watching the colorful shenanigans outside the ring.

All of her attention left the dresser and her upcoming duties when she spied the large picture window. She walked out onto the terrace. The sight took her breath away.

The moon was high in the sky, but she could see the landscape down below. The trees and flowers looked as though they'd been splashed on with watercolors. The blue-green water sparkled under the rays. The sight of the mountains reaching high into the sky took her breath away. In the distance, she saw spires, like something out of a renaissance fair but on a larger scale.

"It's the most beautiful thing I've ever seen," she breathed.

This would be her view? There would be no need for a television here. She would be content, even if she never got to travel beyond this space.

Beryl came up behind her. His arms rested on

either side of her, boxing her in at the railing, but he didn't touch her. "That's Lake Eden down below. Those are the mountains of Gaia. And to the east, is Shephard's Town. I'll take you to see it all soon."

"You will?" She turned to him to see if he meant his words. Poppy knew a lie when she saw it.

Beryl's face was earnest. "Of course. Anything that keeps that expression on your face. You're making my job easy."

"Your job?"

He nodded. "Of providing for you. Protecting you. And ... keeping you pleased."

Poppy's BS-meter ticked over. He'd meant what he'd said about providing and protecting. He hadn't meant to say *pleased*.

Beryl turned back into the room. He pulled out a chair with one hand and put down the platter with the other. He sat down and beckoned her over. Poppy came to him as he bade.

He'd only brought out one chair. She knew he meant for her to sit on his lap. Poppy sat as she was expected to do.

He lifted a morsel of food to her mouth. He blew on it. Tasted it with this tongue. Then he offered it to her.

She should freak out. He was feeding her like she

was a baby. Was that his fetish? Even if it was, she would take the offered food. She was hungry. And she found his care of her arousing.

"Open," he said.

She did as she was told. He placed the morsel on her tongue. His fingers lingered as she closed her mouth and chewed.

"Do you like it?" he asked.

She nodded, smiling as she swallowed.

"What about this?" He placed another morsel on her tongue. It was better than the last. "You like sweet and savory, like me."

"I like salty and sour-y too. I'm not picky."

"Neither am I." He grinned, pleased with that. "Tell me more about you. I want to know everything."

"There's not too much to tell," she said after chewing another bite of food from his fingers. "I'm nobody. I come from nowhere. I haven't done anything."

Beryl's brow lowered along with his hand. From beneath his lowered brow, Poppy spied that bright green of emerald from when he was fighting. He was angry. This time he was angry at her.

"I told you," he said. "I don't like it when you disparage my mate."

There was that word again; *mate*. It had different meanings. In Australia it meant friend. In the animal kingdom, it meant sexual partner. In some romance novels, it meant lifelong partner.

Beryl had to mean she would be his sex partner. So, why all the seduction? Why not just throw her down on the weight bench bed and be done with it? Instead, he was wining and dining her. Well, dining her anyway. The food was so good she felt like it was a drug. Not that she'd ever done any herself.

He offered her more food, still from his fingers. Poppy took what he offered intent on not making him green with anger again. This time her tongue brushed his fingertips. It was an accident. His fingers were so large.

When she pulled her tongue away, Beryl's nostrils flared. He tracked her movement. His eyes glowed emerald as he watched her.

That was not anger this time. She knew the look of sexual desire. He wanted her. Not just the man, but the dragon inside of him.

She'd only seen his wings and a few of his scales. He'd said her spots were scales, like his. But his were beautiful.

She was curious to see his full dragon. She wondered if his scales were as soft as his muscles.

Was his tongue forked? What would his lips feel like against hers?

Beryl leaned in as though he'd heard her questions. She'd been kissed before. It had not been an experience she wanted to repeat. Maybe it would be different with Beryl. She was about to find out. Before his lips could touch hers, a breeze broke them apart. Something blocked out the moon.

Beryl cursed under his breath and turned away from her.

Looking up, she saw another dragon. Not the dark scales of Ilia. This dragon was blue, like a topaz stone. It leaned its scaly arms against the railings in a very human-like fashion. Chin resting on its clawed hands. It appeared to be smiling.

Beryl gave a weary, annoyed sigh. "Poppy, this is my brother, Rhoyl."

Rhoyl lowered his head. He spread his blue wings wide, lifting his body up. He was beautiful, and for a moment, she was mesmerized. Poppy got the impression the dragon wanted to be admired.

"Hey," snapped Beryl in a gruff voice. "Make your offering and get lost. We're in the middle of something here."

Huffs of air escaped the dragon's long nostrils. Was he laughing? Rhoyl opened his mouth and dropped a gem at her foot. It was a large, sparkling topaz.

"It's customary that all my brothers give a new mate a gem," said Beryl. "It's a gift, a pledge. It welcomes you into the family and says you're under his protection."

She'd awakened in the emerald cave, which must belong to Beryl. She'd gotten a jade gem from Elek. Now a topaz from Rhoyl.

Poppy scooped the gem into her hands. It twinkled at her like a fallen star.

Rhoyl bowed his head. He flapped out his wings and flew off into the night. His large body blocked the moon from view before disappearing amongst the trees.

"It's getting late," said Beryl. "You must be tired."

She wasn't. She knew what this was. A ploy to get her into bed. She didn't hesitate when he reached out his hand to her. Time to pay the piper.

At least she didn't think sex would be so terrible with Beryl. She wouldn't make a peep, not a single complaint. She'd simply lay there and let him have her for as long and as rough as he needed to take her. She owed him that for this new life he'd provided for her.

CHAPTER NINE

*P*oppy took Beryl's hand without hesitation. He loved the trust he saw reflected back at him through her gaze. The pads of her fingertips sliding into his palm was a power boost. He squeezed her knuckles, a promise, an oath that he would spend his life building her trust just as he'd built up his bulk.

He nearly missed it. He would've if he weren't watching her so intently for clues to her pleasure spots. Poppy winced when he touched her. Red drained from the tips of her delicate fingers.

"Sorry." He gentled his touch. "Sorry."

"It's fine. I'm okay."

There was that lie again. She didn't trust him. In bodybuilding, many failed to build bulk with high reps, because repeated actions did nothing to trigger muscle growth. Here, he kept doing the same isolated move with his mate. The move was not offering any pleasure or building any trust. He let go of Poppy's hand. He'd need to try a different tactic.

The idea that worked in bodybuilding was that the more strength or weight you used, the more muscle you built. Perhaps he needed to reverse that sentiment. The lighter his touch, the more pleasure for her. He knew exactly where he wanted to try a light touch, and he wouldn't need to rely on his hands to work through the session. But first, he needed to get her comfortable

"Would you like a bath?" asked Beryl.

"No," she said. "I showered before ... before I came here. Can I have a washcloth?"

Washcloth? He didn't have any of the small squares. He didn't even have a towel. He preferred to take a dip in the lake and sun himself dry.

He ripped a piece of his shirt. No matter that it was hard to replace the muscle tee. Serving his mate was worth it.

He walked her to the basin, making sure to keep his hands to himself. Which was hard. He ached to have her in his grasp. She waited while he filled the basin with fresh water from the lake that was pumped in using a system of pipes. Poppy reached for the cloth, but he held it away from her.

"Please," he said. "Let me."

He couldn't resist the chance to care for her in this way. He brought the cloth to her hands, wiping each finger. Gently, he chanted the word over and over again in his mind. Beryl worked her body like a circuit routine. He brought the cloth up and down the flesh of her forearm turning and rotating her limb until her flesh was damp. He lifted the sleeve of her dress, but she stopped his hand.

"Did I hurt you?" he asked.

"No," she said. "It's just … I don't like to be exposed."

Her hands covered the dark scales of her pale skin.

Beryl lifted his gaze from the place she shielded and held her eyes. He knew a little something about the female species. He'd bedded some of the most exotic fairies in the realm. Every single one of them had a complaint about her body. A petal that wasn't bright enough. A stalk that was more willow than vine.

He'd learned early that there was nothing he could say or do to change their minds about themselves. They seemed to like to nitpick for nitpicking's sake.

He wasn't much different. He fussed over the size and shape of his muscles. He spent countless hours in the gym, under weights, pushing himself to achieve the results he wanted.

Poppy didn't need to lift a finger. There were no further steps toward perfection that she could take. He knew she wouldn't believe his words, but maybe he could show her the truth.

She watched, her gaze filling with wonder. He used her awe to his advantage. With one final nudge, her hand slipped away.

He slipped the strap of her dress off. Her breath caught, and she stiffened. Tension went all through her body.

What had he done now? He'd only used his mouth. He checked to make sure his incisors were still sheathed. They were.

"Poppy?"

"Can we just skip the foreplay?"

She moved away from him and went over to the bed. She lay down on her back. Sliding her dress up to her thighs. Her sex was covered with white cloth. The thin scrap was really no barrier at all. What stopped him from pouncing was the lack of arousal coming from between her thighs.

"Isn't this what you really want?" She stared at the ceiling, not meeting his gaze.

He rose, his beast stalking over to his treasure. She seemed tarnished as she lay there.

"Let's just get it over with," she mumbled.

"Get it over with?" he parroted, sitting down on the mattress. His weight caused her hips to sink and her chest to rise. He saw no pointed tips to her breast. There was no hint of arousal. Beryl used his index finger to tilt her chin so that she was looking at him. When she did, her words came out in a rush.

"When you say mate, I'm sure you mean sexual partner. That's how I'll earn my keep here, and I want to stay. I want to go explore like you said we would. I want to eat more of that food. This place is a paradise compared to where I came from. Compared to anywhere back on Earth. If sex is the charge, I'll pay."

Beryl studied her, trying to decipher the meaning of her words. It took him longer than normal because he didn't want to believe the conclusion his mind kept circling back to.

"You don't like sex?" he asked.

"It's fine." Poppy bit her lip. "You can do whatever you want, and I won't make a fuss."

"*Whatever I want?*"

Beryl swallowed. What hit the back of his throat was pure bile. He wanted to go to Valhalla and gut the bastard who had done this to her. Instead, he let his fingers take the worry lines on her brow. But Beryl knew it wasn't because of his touch. He knew he was being gentle. It was someone else's touch that repulsed her.

"I want you to know that *mate* means you are mine. It also means that I am yours. Just the sight of you soothes the beast inside of me. He would do anything to please you. Anything to make you smile, to make you feel safe. Second, what's between us is beyond sexual. I'm prepared to give you my soul, Poppy."

"Oh."

She said the word with reverence. But it was the kind of reverence for a god that was unseen. One she wasn't sure existed.

Beryl leaned down and took her lips. They were stiff but yielding. She parted her mouth for him but remained still.

He was undaunted. Whoever had kissed her

before had not known what they were doing. Beryl was different.

Soon, she kissed him back, parting her lips. He brought his hand to her cheek, tilting her head. His hand slid down her neck to her clavicles. It took everything to break the kiss. The dragon didn't want to stop, but he needed to be certain of something.

"Have you ever …" He didn't like to think about her with another male.

"I have," she confirmed. "I just don't like it. I'm sorry. I'm not any good at it. But I'll hold still while you do your business."

"*Hold still while I do my business*?" Beryl let out a breath.

Of all the things he'd thought of when he finally met his mate, this was not one of them. She didn't like sex? She barely liked being touched. She definitely didn't like being looked at. Both man and beast needed all these things.

With all these obstacles set before his path, how was he going to claim his little mate?

oppy had heard the hosts on traveling shows say many times that traveling changes you. Leaving the spaces you were familiar with brings forth new experiences, new cultures, people, places, sights, tastes, and sounds. The place she wanted to travel the most to was Fiji.

The island was practically a chain of beaches. Beaches with waters of every color from white, to turquoise, to emerald. Looking into Beryl's emerald eyes, she felt like waves were washing over her.

She'd always turned away when Bruce had been over top of her. She couldn't look away from Beryl's dominating figure. There was a spot of gold in his green eyes. Though he was all muscle, there was a bit of baby fat on his cheeks. Poppy wanted to reach up her fingers and test the skin there. But she couldn't. He held her down.

This should be bringing back the horrors of her assault. But the memory was pushed down under the heat of Beryl's chest on hers. His was a welcome weight. The heat coming off him wasn't oppressive. It was comforting, like laying out in a hammock under the sun.

She felt herself swaying on the breeze. She felt cradled in strong arms. And then his lips met hers.

Poppy had never understood the draw of kissing. Most prostitutes didn't bother. It was one thing to have a man put his prick in your body. A condom could protect from most diseases. But there was no protection from the tongue swirling and plunging into the mouth.

Beryl didn't shove his tongue down her throat. His lips brushed hers. The soft touch made her think of standing on the beach. The warm water lapped at her toes, only her toes were her lips. But still, her toes were curling as the water met her ankles because while Beryl's lips were gently lapping at her mouth, his fingers were on her ankles.

Poppy's mind was floating away while her body was drowning in a sea of pleasure. The first brush of his tongue made her body undulate like a wave. Only there was no crash. It was a gentle lapping.

The tide was rising, but not his hands. They rested on her calf, gently kneading. In no rush.

Shouldn't he want to get to the main event? His pants were still on. But he was clearly aroused. She could feel his huge cock pressing into her belly.

Beryl was definitely bigger than Bruce. She wouldn't be able to ignore him while he did his business inside of her. In fact, the more she felt the pull and push of his kisses, the gentle lapping of his fingers, the more she was curious about what he'd feel like inside of her.

She was actually interested in this new experience. She wanted to see this sight. She felt like she was a new person as her lips rose to meet his. She liked the taste of him. She enjoyed his touches. The soft growling sound was a delight to her ears.

Beryl had taken her on a journey. It was a staycation where she got to experience her own body in a new light. She reached out for him, wanting to touch. But he caught her hand.

"I want to be Bruce for you."

"Bruce?" Poppy recoiled from Beryl. Of all the things he could say at this moment, why would he bring up her abusive ex?

"Bruce Bannon, from *The Incredible Hulk*. He was gentle. He was human."

"I don't want a human," she said.

"But you're afraid of me," he said.

Fear was the last thing on her mind. For the first time in her life, Poppy felt desire for a man. That desire didn't cool when she felt something cold wrap around her wrist.

She looked over to see that Beryl had bound her wrists together with a bit of gold chain. He attached the end of the chain to the metal frame on the bed. With her hands over her head, her body was pulled taut. The stretch made wetness pool between her thighs.

"This is for the best," said Beryl. "It will help keep the beast at bay."

"The beast?"

"My dragon. I don't want him to come out while I'm pleasuring you."

"Would he hurt me?"

"No. Never. But he can be hard to control, and I don't want to scare you."

"I'm fine."

Beryl's jaw tensed. It was as though he could hear the small lie in her voice. She wasn't afraid, not of his dragon. Not of the man. But sex was not her forte.

She wanted to please him because she wanted him to keep her. She just knew she wasn't good at this. And Beryl looked like he had expectations of her.

Bruce never did. He'd simply part her thighs, pump a few times, and roll over. It hardly interrupted her day.

But Beryl had kissed her for a solid quarter-hour, and he'd demanded a response. Luckily, he'd done most of the work while she rode his coattails.

He'd bound her to the bed. He couldn't expect too much of her in this position. Could he? She didn't know. What she did know was that he could sense something was wrong.

Poppy schooled her features. "I'm fine," she repeated.

He ran his thick finger over her brow and down to her cheek. "I won't hurt you."

His hand was still on her thigh. It trailed up, under her dress. Her body went rigid when he found her core.

He played around the edges of her sex. Why wasn't he unfastening his pants? Why was she complaining? What he was doing felt amazing. She knew he would stop soon to get his pleasure. She best enjoy it while it lasted.

His thumb made circles around the top of her sex. Poppy began to pant. All the while, Beryl watched her, like she was the travel show, and he was the at-home viewer who was fascinated with the sight before him. And the sounds. Because she was making a lot of unintelligible sounds that weren't English.

Poppy's body went taut as he circled that good spot. She pulled at the bindings on her wrists, wanting to touch him. Her legs shook, and she opened them wider like a wanton.

She was flying, soaring. Colors were brighter. Sounds were crisper. The taste of him on her lips was the best delicacy.

Beryl kissed her while she rode the wave of pleasure. When her body began to settle, he inserted a finger. Poppy gasped. His fingers were certainly bigger than Bruce's little prick. Nope, she couldn't lie still and ignore this.

Poppy cried out as her body resisted. She exhaled, preparing her body. She braced for the invasion of his cock, but he withdrew his finger.

"I'm so sorry, Poppy."

Sorry? For what? She wanted to ask, but she

couldn't form words. And she didn't want to. Beryl was freeing her from her binds and bringing her into the cradle of his arms. If she never got to go anywhere else in her life, if she never got to experience another thing, that ride there was enough.

CHAPTER ELEVEN

He'd never worried about his size before. It had always been a good thing. His large bulk had aided him in fighting. It made him the best. It made the fairies come after him.

But not with his mate.

Poppy was so tiny, so small. She couldn't even take his finger inside of her. He couldn't see how she would ever be able to take his cock, which was definitely thicker than his finger.

He had never worried about this with the fairies. The plantlike women were bendable and easily adjusted to his girth. But Poppy? She was small and made of breakable bones, not vines. How was he going to do this?

She curled into his arms now. Her body was

languid and sated. His was raging, aching to be inside of her, to claim her, and make her his in every sense of the word. But that was just his physical body. His dragon was sedate.

It had been the beast that had stopped when Poppy gasped in pain. The man hadn't heard her. He'd wanted to continue. To stretch her wide with his fingers until she was ready for him.

But she might never be ready for him. His dragon didn't care. It only wanted to hold her and protect her. The man wanted her tiny body fitted snug onto his big one.

His beast growled low in his belly. Beryl agreed that would not be happening anytime soon. His self-control was firmly in place with her. He'd been worried he'd hurt her and not be able to stop himself. But that would never be a concern. He'd die before any harm came to his mate, even if that harm were by his own hand.

She didn't wholly trust him. He knew that by her *fine* answers. But she was coming around. He wouldn't damage that. He held her opinion of him highest.

He massaged the spot on her wrists where the chain had held her still so that he could take his pleasure from her. Most of that pleasure had been in watching her writhe at his touch.

She'd seemed surprised, as though she had not known such pleasure in her own body was possible. But she knew of sex. He knew that, based on the words she'd said.

You can do whatever you want, and I won't make a fuss.

Had she been hurt in her life back on earth? Had she been taken by a male who was unworthy? He had to know so that he knew who he had to kill and dismember.

"Poppy?"

She tilted her head up, eyes drowsy.

"Back on earth, were you ... did someone hurt you?"

She tensed in his arms. He wanted to kick himself. His purpose was to bring her pleasure, not any pain, even if it was only a reminder.

"Yes," she said.

"Was it the man you came here with?"

She sat bolt up. "He's here?"

"No. He's gone to Valhalla. There he will die a thousand deaths at the hands of the Valkyrie. The woman who brought you here, Morrigan. Her kind punishes bad men."

"Oh, you mean Bruce. Well, good. He deserves that."

"Was there another man?"

She looked away. "It doesn't matter. He died a long time ago. My mother killed him. He touched me when I was a child."

Beryl wanted to pull her to him and crush her body into his. But he knew that wouldn't be appreciated. He felt like a complete ass for pouncing on her on their first day together. He should have given her more time. He would now.

He started off the bed. "I'll leave you now."

"Why? Did I do something wrong?"

"No. No, you're perfect. I just forced you into that situation." That was the story of his life. He was a brute. He'd done the same to his mother, to his brothers.

"You didn't force me," Poppy said.

"You didn't want to."

"I told you, you could do what you want."

Beryl shook his head. "It should be the other way around. I should do what you want."

"I liked what you did to me. I'd be okay if you wanted to do it again. Especially the kissing."

He leaned in and kissed her. A soft peck of his lips. A tiny tug of the teeth.

"I'm not gentle by nature," he said. "But I will work hard to be what you need."

She gazed at him quizzically, like she didn't understand his words.

"What do you need?" he asked.

She blinked, as though no one had ever asked her that question.

"You need to sleep."

"Will you stay?" She caught his hand as he rose. "I need you to stay."

Beryl lay back on the mattress. He opened his arms to his mate, and she came to him. Here was where he was proud of his size. She rested her head against his chest, snuggling into him.

"Sleep, little one. Tomorrow you'll meet the rest of my family."

"And then can we go look around?"

"Whatever you wish."

He felt her smile into his chest.

Beryl inhaled and sighed. He would take her wherever she wanted to go. He'd have to stay close to her side as she wasn't claimed, and he'd kill any shifter that dared challenge him for her.

CHAPTER TWELVE

*I*t was all happening so fast.

One moment, Poppy thought she was dead. The next she'd been sacrificed to the most alluring man, who wasn't a man at all. The next, he was fighting for her life. Then she was having her first orgasm ever. And now she was meeting the family.

Things were all out of order. Shouldn't she and Beryl have at least gone out on a date before she was claimed and presented to the rest of the dragon clan?

"We're so glad you're here," said Cardi. The girl was dressed up like Madonna in the '80s with the straps of her bra hanging out of her tight t-shirt, a frilly dress with visible bike shorts, and heels. Her makeup was neon pink, so bright it hurt Poppy's eyes.

Beside her, Chryssie nodded enthusiastically. She was dressed in a simple sundress and sandals with muted makeup. But a moment ago, both women had been on the backs of dragons as they soared through the air around the castle.

Poppy had watched as the two beasts had landed gently with their cargo and then transformed into very naked, very virile males. Thank God, they'd pulled on robes before coming inside.

Kimber and Corun smiled politely at her. Both inclining their heads as though she were royalty. All the while, Beryl stood just behind her, smiling with pride and possession.

Something about the way Beryl looked at her made Poppy feel warm all over. She'd been a man's possession before. She'd never been his treasure. Beryl kept insisting she was both. She knew her duties as a domestic slave. She didn't know how to be something special.

"Let's show you around," said Cardi grabbing her hands. "I'm sure you haven't had a look at anything yet since you've been boinking Beryl."

"Cardi, that's not polite," admonished Chryssie.

Cardi smacked her teeth. "Let me guess, you've seen his horde in the mines?"

"Yes," said Poppy.

"His workout room, probably."

"Yeah."

"And you've seen his bedroom, right?"

"Yes."

"Anything else?"

No, but Poppy hadn't cared to keep her eyes open after the boinking. She'd never wanted a man like this before. Beryl made her feel safe and protected. He made her forget her doubts and fears and worries. With just a lift of his lip, he scared them all away, and she couldn't remember what they'd been.

"Come on then." Cardi tugged at her arm. "These three have business to talk about. We'll take you on a proper tour of your new home."

Chryssie shrugged as if to say no sense in arguing with the girl. Poppy got the sense that Cardi got her way most of the time if not all of it. Why else would she walk around like she was stuck in the eighties when she was clearly grown.

Before she could traipse after Cardi, Beryl wrapped his large hand around her neck. He pulled her in for a breath-stealing kiss. When he let her up for air, she colored with embarrassment. She looked to the side to see Corun kissing Chryssie tenderly. He brushed a hand over her belly as he did so.

Turning to Kimber and Cardi, Poppy saw Cardi take a step toward Kimber. The male narrowed his gaze in disapproval and put up his hand.

"Behave," Kimber said in a gravelly voice.

Cardi's face transformed into the pinched look of a child who was about to throw a tantrum. But she minded him and took Poppy's hand again. The three women went down one hall as the men went down another.

The further she got away from Beryl, the more bereft Poppy felt. She'd only known the man for a half a day, and she felt lost without him. How had that happened?

"This is the man cave," said Cardi.

She opened a door to reveal gaming consoles and large screen televisions. Ilia sat on the couch, playing one of the games. He stood at the women's approach. When he saw Poppy, his eyes slammed down.

"What did you do?" asked Cardi.

To Poppy, she looked like a little sister chastising an older brother.

"I challenged Beryl for her."

"Well, of course, you did." Cardi turned back to

Poppy. "It's how they do things here. Their dad challenged Kimber for me."

"Ilia nearly burned me to a crisp in the process," said Poppy.

Cardi narrowed her gaze at Ilia. "You know what to do."

Ilia came before Poppy and dropped to his knees. "'God, I'm so pathetic. Don't you ever, ever compare yourself to me, okay. You got everything, and I got shit. Fuckin' Rapunzel, right? School would probably fuckin' shut down if you didn't show up.'"

Poppy took a step back. She looked up at the other girls. Chryssie sighed and shook her head. Cardi nodded at Ilia approvingly.

"What's happening?" Poppy asked.

"He's apologizing," said Cardi.

"It's Bender talking to Claire," said Chryssie as though Poppy was supposed to know what that meant. "You know, from *The Breakfast Club*. Just let him get it out."

"'Screws fall out all the time'," Ilia continued. "'The world is an imperfect place.'"

He stood and offered her a jade gem. Poppy hesitated for a second, but then took the gem. The smooth stone was heavy in her hand.

"Um, thank you," said Poppy. "And you're forgiven. I don't think you were trying to kill me."

"I was trying to claim you. I called dibs on the next sacrifice, but Beryl didn't respect the dibs. That's not sportsmanlike."

Poppy wasn't sure how to respond to that. She'd come from a world where dollars bought dibs. She was now an object of dibs. At least she was clear that Beryl had no intention of sharing her with anyone.

"You're family now," said Ilia. "And I will protect you with my life as you're now my sister."

"Your sister?"

"Of course. You're the mate of my brother."

Chryssie came and ducked under Ilia's arms. "They may seem scary at first, but they are the sweetest guys."

"Don't call me sweet," said Ilia. "It messes with my street cred."

"There are no streets here," said Chryssie. "Everyone walks, runs, or flies."

"Everyone?" asked Poppy. "There are other people here?"

"Humans? No. Fairies, lions, wolves, bears, Valkyries, yes."

"What?"

"Didn't Beryl explain this? This is the Garden of

Eden. The place where God, who is actually a woman, did her biological experiments. You want to see?"

Did Poppy, who'd never been anywhere in the world, want to see a magical land of creatures?

"Yes."

"You should wait for your mates," said Ilia.

"They're in a boring meeting," said Cardi.

"What? No one told me," huffed Ilia. He turned and stormed out of the room.

"Besides, those two are claimed," Cardi said to Ilia's retreating back. "And no one will touch me because I'm Kimber's. We'll be fine."

CHAPTER THIRTEEN

"Congratulations, brother."

Kimber clapped Beryl on the back. The praise felt good coming from his elder brother. Kimber had often sighed and pinched the bridge of his nose as a result of Beryl's actions with fairies, or fighting with other shifters in the realm, or fighting with his brothers in the castle. Or fighting in general.

"Yes," said Corun. "She is a beautiful specimen. And it looks as though she didn't try to kill you. That's a bonus."

"Poppy is everything I could ever have imagined in a mate. Smart, beautiful, and strong in body and mind." Even though she was a bit damaged by what the men of her world had put her through.

Inside his gut, the dragon ground his molars.

Poppy was here now, with him. No other male would ever lay a finger on her. Not if he wanted to keep it attached to his body.

"How much did you pay for her?" Kimber's question was crass, but as the eldest, it was his responsibility to mind the horde of their treasure.

"A sacrifice is priceless," Beryl hedged.

Corun's usually serious face cracked a smile at Beryl's evasive answer. He'd given up his entire stash of rubies to keep his bride. At first, Corun had sent Chryssie back to the world beyond the Veil thinking it would save her from the dragon babies growing in her belly. Only to find that she would surely die back on earth with the fire that ran through her blood. He'd gone to get her. The price for a dragon entering the human world was death. However, he'd skirted that price tag by offering up his entire treasure to the Valkyries. The fierce warriors had squealed like newly hatched birds at shiny beads and left the mines with more than they could carry in gems.

Beryl had thought Corun's actions mad at the time. But he also adored Chryssie and, if the need had arisen, he would've pitched in his own treasure to keep her with them. Now, he had a treasure of his own.

Kimber, on the other hand, was all business. He

ran their mining operation with precision, insisting each of his brothers reach a weekly quota. He was the Vince McMahon of the mines. Having taken over the business from their father after the old dragon's demise, Kimber had exploded the family income. But unlike McMahon, Kimber was not a showman. He stayed behind the scenes and counted the money. Now, his diamond-hard glare flashed at Beryl to know the new price tag.

"I told the Valkyrie to take what she wanted," said Beryl. "I didn't look to see what she took."

Kimber sighed, pinching the bridge of his nose. When he pulled his hand away, the spot remained red. That spot got a lot of attention between his brothers, his mate, and his responsibilities in the Veil.

"We are already down by a lot with Corun starting from scratch." When he'd learned about Corun's negotiations with the Valkyries, he'd grumbled for weeks. "Elek and Ilia are barely pulling their weight. Rhoyl spends his days sunbathing and his nights hunting, so he is mostly useless. And then there's this, I hear that you nearly killed one of Leona's cubs."

Beryl twisted his lip. He had been hoping to get away with his brother not knowing that bit of information. Kimber knew about Beryl's participation in the fights Leona organized. Beryl was loud and proud of his winnings. Except for what happened last night with Leander.

"My beast got out of control," he said.

"When will you learn that when you go Hulk, it's me that has to go behind and Bannon things up."

When they'd watched the *Incredible Hulk* television shows on tape, Kimber and Corun had always identified with the cunning scientist, while each of the triplets had been fascinated by the green behemoth. Of course, he would take Bannon's side. Beryl long suspected his big brother had cheered for Andre the Giant over Hulk Hogan in their last wrestling match.

"It won't happen again," said Beryl. "I have no need to go green. I've mated. My hulking beast is calm now."

His beast hadn't raised its head since coming from between Poppy's thighs. For the first time since he was a fledgling, Beryl hadn't felt the need to run or lift a weight or push his body in any way physical. All he wanted to do was find his mate and hold her close.

"Doesn't change the fact that Leona is

demanding restitution for the life-threatening injury of her cub," said Kimber.

"Leander is not a cub," Beryl protested. "He's a full-grown lion. And he's alive. I've done worse to the two of you."

"Be that as it may, she went to the Valkyries and petitioned. They agreed. You have been fined."

"How much?" Beryl had begun to suspect that Leona's operation might be more than a way to get the aggression out of her own sons. They all knew the only thing that would settle a shifter male was a mate. The fights were bringing in coin, gems, and precious metals from those coming to watch and the bets taking place. Currency given to the Valkyries was the only current way to get mates into the Veil.

Kimber handed Beryl a piece of parchment with a figure written at the center. Beryl's eyes bugged out at the amount written there.

"That's insanity," Beryl said. Now he pinched the bridge between his nose.

"It will take you two weeks to mine that amount," Corun said. His brother could calculate sums quickly and easily in his head.

"You best get to work," said Kimber.

"Fine," grumbled Beryl. "I'll get it all. Can I at least get to work after I claim my mate?"

"You haven't claimed her yet?" Kimber and Corun said in unison.

"She just got here." Beryl shrugged.

Kimber and Corun looked at each other. Kimber pinched his lips. Corun inhaled deeply.

"I marked her," said Beryl. "But ... she's very small."

"You won't break her," said Corun. "The human body is made to stretch."

"Tell that to our mothers," said Beryl.

A low growl started in the throats of both males. The topic of their mothers was a sore spot because neither woman had lived to see their sons grow. They'd all been born into this world as murderers. But Beryl was the worst.

He had ripped his mother to shreds on his exit. Of course, he hadn't been conscious of his actions as a whelp. But his father had made his son's deeds plain as soon as he was old enough to understand.

Not only had Beryl killed his mother on entry into the world, he'd also nearly starved his brothers while in the womb. That was why Ilia was born a runt, and Rhoyl barely had the strength to stay in human form.

"Sex is different," said Corun.

Beryl didn't want to have this talk with his brothers. "I just need time. I don't want to hurt her."

"Claiming her should be your first priority," said Kimber. "With all the work we'll need to do to catch up, and get ahead, especially with two men down and two newlyweds, and hatchlings on the way, and more sacrifices likely to arrive soon. I doubt we'll ever get ahead."

"At least more dragons will be born," said Corun. "We are no longer in danger of being the last of our kind."

"Especially if Kimber ever claims Cardi," said Beryl.

Kimber grimaced. "She's still a child."

"Children don't have those kinds of curves, brother," said Beryl.

Kimber's growl shook the floorboards. "Do not speak of her in that way."

"Children also don't elicit the kind of response from their mates," said Corun.

Kimber turned away from both of his brothers. Beryl had never understood why his brother had waited so long to claim his mate. He'd marked her, but he had never taken her to bed for the claiming.

Cardi had been a child when she'd first come, only seventeen years old in her time. No one would touch a young girl not ready for claiming. Time moved differently behind the Veil. It had been over thirty years on the other side, but in that time, Cardi had aged into a mature young woman. Still, Kimber wouldn't claim her.

Luckily, everyone knew and accepted that she was his. No one would touch her. And if they did, they'd have to face down the most powerful dragon in the realm.

No one knew Poppy or Beryl's dibs on her. Claiming her would be necessary for her to move through the town without any of the lions, bears, or wolves trying to stake their own claim.

"I see you didn't wait for me to start this meeting." Ilia came to stand in the center of the room, giving each of his brothers what Cardi called the stank eye.

"We're not having a meeting," said Corun.

"Talking behind my back, then?" said Ilia.

"Beryl was simply telling us about his new mate," said Kimber. "You already met her."

Ilia's face pinched into a grimace. "I met her second, but I called dibs first."

Beryl gave his brother a stinky eye of his own before turning his back. "I'm not sticking around for this. If you need me, I'll be with my mate. Where did you leave the girls, Ilia?"

"I didn't leave them anywhere. They went into town."

The hairs at the back of Beryl's neck lifted. A shiver of ice went down his spine. His wings were already unfurling before he leaped out the window to get to his mate before she could set foot in town and be scented by any other male.

CHAPTER FOURTEEN

For a woman who had never been anywhere, this was one hell of a first trip outside the known. Poppy always thought she'd liked small places. That she liked her world confined. Being out in the open of the Veil, she realized how wrong she was.

This place was unreal. It was as though she was walking through a television screen, in high definition. The colors of the trees were so vibrant and bright. Looking up at the sky, she would've sworn she was looking at the underside of a crystal ball because it was so clear blue. It looked as though someone had dropped a box of crayons that had melted over the canvass.

Her imagination was having trouble believing

what her eyes were telling her. She made sure to walk on the graveled paths because the plants opened their eyes and looked up at her. A few lifted their leaves and waved.

"You know how they say the trees have ears," said Chryssie. "Well, once upon a time, that was true. Here it still is true."

Poppy watched willowy plants walk around on sturdy stems. Some looked more human than plant. A few even had wings like butterflies.

Chryssie and Cardi explained how plants were the first living things to evolve on land. When they did, they were sentient. The Goddess tinkered with their DNA until they could communicate with Her and with each other. There were some plants that uprooted themselves and walked on their stalks during the day, sinking back into the rich earth each night to get sustenance. Those plants, or fairies as they liked to call themselves, crossed out of the garden and into the world of other living beings.

Many of Her original creations still lived here in the garden. Plants weren't the only beings the Goddess tinkered with. She'd experimented with what humans knew as the dinosaurs. That's how dragon shifters came to be. She'd also tried to make men out of wolves, lions, and bears.

The architecture within the Veil was also breathtaking. Many structures were built out of the surrounding landscape. There were a few pyramids, many dome-like structures, but mostly massive rectangular structures that resembled the buildings of today's world. Only not many went much higher than three stories. That allowed for clear views of the pristine, mostly untouched land that went on as far as Poppy could see.

"So, what part of the world are we actually in?" asked Poppy.

"You can't think of it like that," said Cardi. "We're on another plane of existence. You can access just about any part of the world from this point."

"So, I could go anywhere on the Earth from here?" asked Poppy.

Anywhere she wanted? Like Montenegro, or Malta, or even Miami?

"Yup," said Cardi. "Humans can go out and in because they can exist in both realms. Fairies, too."

"Wow," sighed Poppy, feeling that the world was truly her oyster. "So, Beryl and I could take a vacation without flying?" Or maybe he would fly her on his back like Corun and Kimber had flown Cardi. She'd never been on a plane, but she would love to travel by dragon.

"Dragons can't leave," said Chryssie. "They're trapped here."

"Trapped? Why?" asked Poppy.

"The Goddess didn't create dragon shifters to live in both worlds," said Chryssie. "If they cross over the Veil into the human world, they'll get sick and die. That's why we all were sick when we lived there."

Chryssie eyed Poppy's arm. There was a spot peeking out at the edge of the T-shirt she'd pulled on this morning. Poppy was dressed in a *Frankie Says Relax* t-shirt, black leggings, and Puma sneakers that were a size too small. Poppy tugged at the sleeve of the shirt, but it wouldn't stretch enough to cover her.

"It's okay." Chryssie put her hand over Poppy's. "You're one of us."

One of us. Poppy had never belonged to anyone that hadn't been her blood, like her mother. Or a pimp that used her, like Bruce.

"There's fire in your blood," said Chryssie. "There's fire in our blood, too. We're descendants of dragons."

"Yeah, there was a sacrifice who escaped," Cardi chimed in. "She made it back across the Veil, but she was preggers. Had two sons. For some reason, the sons only had girls."

"Because only the daughters survived," said Chryssie. "You know, girl power and all."

"Damn straight," said Cardi, lifting her hand for a high five from both of them.

Poppy slapped her new friend's hand. The smack of palms sent a shock of power through Poppy. Her shirt sleeve slipped higher. She didn't reach to pull it back down.

"Anyway," Chryssie continued. "We weren't meant to survive in that world. We were meant to be here. This is where we belong."

For the first time in her life, Poppy did feel like she belonged. She belonged with these two women. Not just because they were redheads. Not just because they'd both had incurable diseases. Because she sensed they'd been outcasts and under-valued in their old life. But here, they were all treasures.

"We're here," announced Cardi. "Thank the Goddess because I'm starved. This is my favorite place to eat in all the Veil. I come here all the time when Kimber lets me off his leash."

Poppy looked up to see a building that looked like a barn. The exterior was comprised of large, wooden slates. Over the door was emblazoned God's Teet.

The large double doors stood wide open with

delectable scents and raucous laughter wafting out. Inside, Poppy saw more flower people. White lilies with purple eyes and green limbs. Stout shrubby males with green bushy hair.

In the far back of the room was a cage. There was a tall male fairy mopping the floors. The water he used was tinged red like he'd been mopping up blood.

"Are you sure it's safe here?"

Cardi looked over toward the direction of Poppy's gaze. "Oh, that. That's where they hold the cage matches."

Cage matches? She'd seen those on television when Bruce had guests over. The men were bare-chested and barefooted. They'd be locked inside a cage with a referee who let them beat each other to a bloody pulp. Poppy could never watch.

"Your boy, Beryl, is the title champion of the Veil," said Cardi.

Beryl? He fought in that thing. Was that his blood? Or did he bleed others?

"Kimber won't let me come to see those either. Thinks it's not appropriate for someone my age like I'm twelve or something."

Cardi walked up to a table of fairies. She put her

hands on her hips and stared. After five seconds, the table cleared.

She turned back to Chryssie and Poppy with a glint in her eyes. "It's good to be the queen."

"We're royalty?" Poppy asked, taking one of the vacated seats.

"Pretty much," said Poppy. "Dragons are at the top of the food chain here. Well, aside from the Valkyries."

"Kimber is the king?"

Cardi shrugged one shoulder. "He's the oldest and the strongest."

Poppy twisted her lip. From the looks of the dragon shifters, she would've said that her Beryl was the strongest. But she didn't voice this opinion. Not to her first-ever friends. But Chryssie caught her eye, like she knew what Poppy was thinking, and winked.

"How long have you both been here?" Poppy asked.

"I've been here about two months in human time," said Chryssie. "But time moves differently on this side of the Veil. It's probably been half a year or so. Cardi's been here a lot longer."

Cardi dressed like she was from thirty years ago. But she didn't look a day over twenty.

"I've been dying to know something," said Cardi.

"Back on the other side, did Zach and Kelly actually get married?"

"Who?" asked Poppy.

"From *Saved by the Bell*," said Chryssie.

"Oh, yeah. After *The College Years* spin-off show. There was a prime time special like ten years ago and—"

"No." Cardi put her hands over her ears. "Don't tell me anymore. I don't want to know. Not good to know your future. Doc Brown taught us that in *Back to the Future*."

"Well, yeah," said Chryssie. "But in the second movie they—"

Cardi dropped her hands from her ears. "There's a second *Back to the Future* movie?"

Poppy decided not to tell her that the franchise had developed into a trilogy.

The light in the room dimmed. Poppy looked over to see two large males blocking the sun. For a moment, she thought one of them might be Beryl. But both of the males sported a thick mane of blond hair.

"Great," sighed Cardi. "Here comes trouble. Let me go and get our drinks before the lions lap up every drop."

She rose from her chair and began to make her

way toward the bar. But one of the massive men—or lion men—stepped in her path.

"Mmm," the lion purred. The man was shirtless, sporting a hairy, golden chest. "Nothing like the smell of sweetmeat in the afternoon."

"Gag me with a spoon, Ari," Cardi said with a roll of her eyes and flip of her hair.

"Let her alone, Ari," said the lion beside him. The man could've been Ari's twin, except his mane was trimmed to rest just above his shoulders, where Ari's ran down his back. "You know who she belongs to and what he'll do if he finds out you touched her."

"Shut it, Izem." Ari brushed the other man's words aside. "We both can smell that that limp dick dragon still hasn't plucked her petals yet."

The thing about being a redhead was that it was hard to hide your emotions. Embarrassment, anger, joy they all showed up on your face in splotches of red. Cardi looked like a beet. But she stood her ground in front of the two large males. It was clear to Poppy that that wasn't fear in her wide eyes, it was a mixture of shame and anger.

"What goes on with my petals is none of your business, you overgrown meat sack. Now get out of my way, or tomorrow you'll wake up with your pretty hair permed."

It was David staring down Goliath. Cardi was tiny in comparison to the lions. But Ari blinked first.

Poppy knew two things in that moment. One, she would never piss off Cardi. Two, she wanted to be just like Cardi when she grew up.

Ari stepped aside. The sound of his molars grinding and his fists clenching filled the room as he did so. Izem also took a step back, but he did it with a grin.

Cardi stepped away from them. The moment she did, a breeze wafted through the doors. It lifted Poppy's hair. The lions' noses lifted into the air as well. When the dust in the air settled, two sets of glowing eyes landed on Poppy.

"An unclaimed human?" Ari's voice was low, deep, predatory.

Poppy felt like a gazelle out in the Sahara the moment after it was spotted with nowhere to run. Chryssie took her hand under the table. Her face set into fierce lines.

"She's not unclaimed," said Cardi, marching back into the fray and putting her small body between Poppy and the lions. "This is Beryl's new mate. He claimed her last night. Right, Poppy?"

Poppy didn't have to say anything. Her redhead

traits were betraying her all over her cheeks and her neck. Even her arms were bright red.

"Beryl bit me." She was so embarrassed to admit that much. She definitely wasn't telling them what else they got up to, not even under the duress of being eaten by one of these lions.

"And he boinked you," Cardi encouraged. "Right?"

"Um ..."

Cardi whirled around to face Poppy. "'Um' is not the right answer in this situation."

"We did ... stuff ..."

"But you haven't been boinked? Did he insert tab B into slot A?"

Poppy opened her mouth and then closed it. Once again, she had no need to answer. It was clear they all saw red.

CHAPTER FIFTEEN

Beryl pushed his wings hard. His shoulders ached as he carried his heavy load through the air, going faster than was prudent. He ignored the pain in his back. He ignored the strain of his wings.

No pain, no gain, and he had to gain on getting to Poppy.

Even now, a lion could be sniffing at her hide. A wolf might be flashing its canines. Thank the Goddess the bears were still sleeping.

He caught a whiff of her on the wind. She was close. The tendrils of her delicate scent erased the burn from his muscles. Beryl pushed harder.

Shephard's Town wasn't that big. There were few establishments to purchase clothing, food, and supplies. The inhabitants of the Veil still practiced the ancient art of bartering. It was mainly the Valkyries who coveted gemstones. Because the daughters of the Goddess were able to travel outside of the Veil and collect prized items, many of the beings began to trade in precious metals as well.

It was another reason the girls should be left alone. No one wanted to anger the dragons on account of their tempers. But also because everyone wanted access to gems.

Unfortunately, the knowledge that others *shouldn't* bother Cardi, Chryssie, or Poppy wasn't enough. Human women were an item coveted more than any sustenance, more than any gem. Especially by other male shifters.

Now inside the town's boundaries, Beryl didn't bother following his nose. He knew exactly where Cardi would take them. The only place truly worth her time. Sure enough, he saw the girls through the open double doors of God's Teet as he landed.

Beryl's powerful thighs hit the ground. Claws dug into the rich soil. Smoke curled from his nostrils as he rushed toward the doors. The dragon gave him back his skin when it realized he couldn't fit into the doors. Beryl burst into the bar, naked as the day he was born. Dragons didn't typically shift out in public. But desperate times and all.

Ari was at her front. Izem was at her back. Cardi stepped in front of Ari wagging her finger as though the lion would heel to a human. For a moment, Beryl thought Ari might.

After an inhale, he dropped all consideration of letting Cardi put the lions in their place. Beryl smelled fear on his mate. His dragon scratched at his skin to get back out.

"Back up off her now." Beryl still had his body, but the beast had taken back his voice.

Poppy's gaze darted immediately to him. Beryl was gratified that her gaze filled with relief. But the smell of fear came back when Ari cuffed her upper arms.

"She's not claimed," the lion said. "How do we even know she wants you."

"She bears my mark." Beryl's vision was a green so dark, he could barely make out what was around him. "She belongs to me."

"A mark means nothing. You just pissed on her leg. You haven't moved in."

Lions were big males. Not as big as him. But one would rip Poppy apart if not careful. Ari wasn't the most careful of males. He'd broken many of Beryl's toys when he'd come over to play as a cub; his Optimus Prime Battle Convoy for one. In retaliation, Beryl ripped the head off Ari's prized Lion-O action figure. With his clumsy paws, Ari could break Poppy.

Beryl was fast losing the ability to think, to reason. All that mattered was getting to Poppy and getting Ari's hands off her. He was tainting her perfect skin with his fur.

Anger rippled over his muscles. Everything in his sight turned green. Puffs of air curled out of his nostrils like toxic gamma rays. He curled his fists into hammers, ready to smash his way to her.

"You have my mate behind you," came a calm voice.

Beryl didn't turn to see Kimber standing beside him. His brother had been on his tail as he'd cut through the sky. He knew that Corun was at his other side. Ilia was standing just outside the door along with Rhoyl. The only one who'd stayed home was Elek to stand guard over the castle, their horde, and his mother.

Some of the bluster went out of Ari at the sight of the fierce weyr of dragons. Beryl would have liked to think he alone inspired Ari's lowered tone. But even he could feel the power in his brother's low voice.

"For the love of the Goddess, calm down children."

A collective breath of relief was taken at the appearance of Leona. Everyone except Beryl. His fists curled into hammers, waiting for the moment he could pound Ari's jaw permanently closed.

"Boys, let the females go."

"I didn't do anything," said Izem.

Leona's bright gaze cut to Izem. With just a lift of her brow, she communicated volumes.

"But, Mama," whined Ari.

Leona made a hissing sound like an angry cat. Ari dropped his arms from blocking the girls' way.

"We didn't touch your mate, Kimber," said Izem. "Everyone knows Cardi's yours, even if you still haven't claimed her."

"Wonder if he even wants to," muttered Cardi.

Beside her, Izem cocked his head toward her, his bushy brow raised up like a question mark.

"He hasn't even kissed me," Cardi said as though the lion's brow had asked her a direct question.

Izem's brows lowered. His gaze narrowed, focusing on Cardi's lips.

Beryl had always thought Izem one of the smarter cubs. Looks like he was wrong. The male clearly had a death wish.

"Cardinal," Kimber warned.

But Cardi wasn't cowed. She was never cowed. She crossed her arms over her chest and huffed as she crossed the distance to them. When she reached Kimber, he tucked her behind him.

"We didn't touch yours either, Corun," said Izem. "She's clearly been claimed. Felicitations on the cubs."

Corun was unmoved. His upper lip remained curled. His hard glare persisted on the lion shifters.

Chryssie rushed into Corun's arms. He placed his hand on her belly and his lips in her hair. All the while, his gaze never left the lions.

Poppy didn't follow the girls. Her gaze was trained on the ground. She was shaking, but she didn't attempt to move, to flee, to run to the safety of Beryl's arms.

"She's not coming to you," said Ari. "That tells me she's fair game."

Poppy stood there, trembling like a leaf in a light breeze. Her face was ashen. He could smell the cold sweat trickling down her brow. She was terrified.

As fast as a pickax could strike stone, Beryl was on Ari. "What did you do to her?"

But Ari couldn't answer. Beryl's paw was wrapped tightly around the lion's windpipe. Ari's claws dug into Beryl's wrists, but Beryl felt nothing but ire for the lion.

All around him, he heard Kimber's voice, Leona's voice, telling him to let Ari go. He ignored them all. It was the tiniest of whimpers that loosened his grip.

Poppy had lifted her gaze. She was staring at him, her lips and chin trembling. Her eyes blinked rapidly; trying to see things clearly, trying to erase what she was seeing, he had not a clue. All that mattered was soothing the dismay from her perfect brow.

In a sea of green, she was the one bright light. He dropped his hold on Ari. The lion fell to the ground in a loud thunk. Beryl enfolded his mate in his arms.

He wrapped her up tight, needing to put his scent on her immediately. His beast was still riled up and needing blood, but its first priority was her, his mate. Poppy was tense in his arms. Her eyes unseeing. Her chin stiff.

Had Ari left a scar, a mark? If he had, heads would roll no matter the custom.

"Beryl, dear, try not to leave your toys around without your name on them if you don't want others to claim them," Leona said.

Izem's lip curled in a smirk. Around the bar, there were a few other chuckles. Beryl took a deep breath, breathing in Poppy's scent. She still wasn't looking at him. Her large eyes were glossed over, as though only her body was present.

"What did you do to her?" growled Beryl.

"Gave her an option," said Ari from the floor. The lion had a few brain cells, he hadn't gotten up from where Beryl had dropped him. "I think she's thinking about it."

Finally, Poppy's gaze lifted. Pure terror was reflected back at him. He would rip Ari's head off.

Man and beast were in agreement. "I'm going to kill you."

"Challenge accepted," grinned Ari. His canines were out, along with his claws.

"No," bellowed Kimber. Once again, everyone in the bar stopped what they were doing. Hearing the guttural roar of the most powerful dragon in the land turned them all as still as stones. "We do not practice the ways of our fathers. We are better men than that."

Izem nodded, taking a step back.

Ari sneered, biting at the top of his lip as though he were considering the depths of his character.

Beryl didn't have to think. "He touched my mate. I want his blood."

"Beryl—"

Beryl wasn't listening anymore. He scooped Poppy into his arms, stepped through the door, and ran with his precious cargo secured in his arms.

"Remember the old rules," he heard Leona call faintly, "don't taint the prize before she's won."

CHAPTER SIXTEEN

She couldn't catch her breath. Poppy's heart was pounding so hard that her lungs couldn't fill. She tried to open her mouth and take in air, but tremors ran all over her body, making her head droop.

Her forehead landed on something firm but soft. The smell of sweat and earth hit the back of her nose, knocking some sense back into her. It was the smell of safety. It was the smell of Beryl.

He'd come for her. Taken her from the clutches of that man, that beast, who had touched her. The lion shifter had planned to take her against her will.

No, not against her will.

Poppy hadn't resisted Ari. She'd played possum like she'd always done with the men who barged into her life. She hadn't fought the man who'd climbed onto her as a child. She'd never once said no to Bruce. If Cardi and Chryssie hadn't stood up for her, if Beryl hadn't come for her, would Poppy have let the lions take her?

God, she was so pathetic. So weak. She was not going to survive in this world where women actually had to speak up or get eaten. If she wanted to stay with Beryl, if he even still wanted such a pitiful excuse for a woman, she'd have to find her voice.

He ran with her in his arms. He went so fast the scenery around her was a blur. Even though he was the one running, she was out of breath.

"Beryl, please. Please, stop."

He came to an immediate halt. It was almost cartoonish the way his feet pumped to a stop and dirt kicked up around them. But neither of them were in a laughing mood.

They were out in the middle of nowhere. Poppy couldn't see the town from this distance. She could barely make out the castle up in the mountains either.

Beryl tugged at the bottom of her shirt, lifting it up and exposing her skin. He lifted her shirt over her head, leaving her breasts exposed. The only bras available in the stash of clothes he'd shown her earlier had been a few sizes too small, so she'd gone without. Poppy crossed her arms over herself. Beryl shoved her hands out of the way and ran his hands over her skin.

"Beryl, please," she begged.

He ignored her pleas. His hands rubbed roughly over her spots. But it wasn't sexual. Poppy knew what a sexual advance felt like. This was something different.

"Did he hurt you?" Beryl demanded. "Did he leave a mark?"

"What?"

"Ari. That hairy bastard. I'll kill him, revive him, and then kill him again."

"No. I don't think so."

Apparently, Beryl was unconvinced. His fingers combed every inch of her skin, looking for a hint of damage.

"It's fine," she said. "I'm fine."

That brought his head up. His gaze flashed on her, emerald shining bright in the afternoon sun. "Don't lie to me. You are not fine."

The anger in his voice shrank her down into her shoes. His mouth, which had given her so much pleasure last night, turned cruel. The dream of a man showing her kindness, maybe even showing her love, died before her eyes. Poppy brought her hands up to her face, to protect herself from the sight of the total transformation.

"You think I would strike you?"

She didn't answer. She didn't move her hands from her face. She'd known it was too good to be true.

He was too good. It couldn't be true. All men were beasts.

Beryl fought in cage matches; bloody ones. He'd made his own brother bleed the day she got here. He'd wrapped his hands around Ari's neck and watched him lose his air. He would hurt her just like Bruce, just like her abuser, just like that lion had intended to.

She would take it like she always did. She needed to figure out how to keep Beryl happy, how to not tug on the anger trigger like she'd just done. She wasn't under any illusion that it would never happen again. There were always minefields in a relationship.

"I would never hurt you," he said.

"I know," Poppy said.

It was strange, though. Beryl sounded sincere. She could always hear the lie in Bruce's voice. Bruce's voice would go softer with deceit. Like it was a secret, and since he'd only told her, he didn't have to keep it.

But Beryl was loud with his dishonesty. He fairly shouted the words. Loud enough that they could have been heard back at the bar by everyone present.

Poppy kept her voice quiet as she continued to placate him. "It was my fault."

"Your fault?" His face contorted into deeper angry lines.

Shit. Wrong move. She braced herself for an explosion.

Beryl's hands came to her cheek. His touch was gentle, reverent. He cupped her face with prayer hands. His thick fingers would've made the steeple except her face was in the way.

"You should have waited for me," he said, his voice quieter now.

Poppy no longer thought he would hit her. Though she preferred the hitting to the verbal abuse. Physical bruises healed quicker than the internal ones. She knew Beryl's words would hurt.

"You are precious to me," he continued his assault. "There are dangerous things in this world. I need to be there to protect you from them. It's my job, my responsibility. If anything had happened to you—"

Beryl dropped his hands and turned away from her. His shoulders caved in as though someone had sucker-punched him. A guttural roar tore from his throat.

Poppy stumbled at the loss of his hands holding her. Not one of his words had lashed out to wound her. He seemed angry at himself, not her.

"I shouldn't blame you," he said. "You didn't know any better. You didn't know that going out into this world that other males would look at you as though you were fair game."

He turned back to her. His cheeks were ruddy, as though shame had crept up there. His chin dropped to his chest as though it were weighed down by guilt.

"Forgive me," he said, his voice a plea.

"Forgive you?" Poppy parroted. Her mind whirled.

But each direction she turned she couldn't make sense of her predicament. Where were the punishing words to make her bleed internally? Why was the blame not heavy on her shoulders?

"It's my fault," Beryl said, taking cautious steps towards her. "I didn't claim you."

"Claim me?" Poppy brought her hand to her

shoulder where Beryl's bite had raised the skin there.

"That's a mark." Beryl's hand covered hers. "Claiming is ... more."

"Do you want to claim me?"

"I *will* claim you."

His words were vehement. But she didn't cringe at his tone. She didn't back away from the dangerous glint in his eyes. Somehow, she knew it wasn't directed at her.

"I will rip Ari's head off before he can get his paws anywhere near you."

Right. The fight. There was going to be a fight. And she was the prize.

All that had slipped her mind. Because it made no sense. She was nothing special.

"Beryl, I don't want you to fight for me."

"You are mine," he growled. Again loudly. Whispering didn't seem to be in Beryl's repertoire. He must not have learned about the inside voice as a child.

Still, she'd watched enough daytime talk shows to know that those were the words of a possessive male. For a woman who had been in an abusive relationship most of her life, possessive was a great upgrade from abusive.

"It's just that, I don't want you to get yourself hurt," Poppy said. "Especially not for me."

Beryl's lips pressed tight. His throat worked, Adam's apple bobbing up and down as though something was stuck there. "You don't think I'm strong enough to protect you?"

"What? No. That's not what I said."

His head raised, and the corners of his mouth lifted at her words. This was good. She'd figured out another way to please him. Most men were easily flattered. Luckily, she didn't have to stretch the truth with Beryl.

"I believe you could take that lion man down. Probably both of them."

Now his chest puffed up. He rested his fists on his hips like she'd seen bodybuilders do in their poses. It would've been comical if he wasn't so damn sexy.

"But the fight's not worth it," she said. "I'm not worth it."

Beryl's eyes flashed emerald. He was on her before she finished her statement. His large hand wrapped around her neck. His fingers tugging her hair until her head was bent back.

She should be scared. She should be terrified.

Instead, she felt heat pooling between her thighs. Her nipples pulled into two aching points.

"What did I say about talking bad about my treasure?"

Poppy was wrong. Beryl did have an inside voice. His growl was so low it reverberated in the bones of her spine, turning her knees to mush.

"I said I would punish you, didn't I?"

A cool sensation washed over Poppy. It wasn't fear. It was anticipation.

Beryl yanked her head to his, capturing her mouth in a searing kiss. Poppy had been punched, kicked, spat upon, degraded until her ears burned from the insults. This punishment topped all that abuse.

Before, she'd kept a small part of herself away from the abusive men in her life. With Beryl, that wouldn't be possible. With his every touch, his every word, his every glance, he stole a piece of her armor and slipped into her heart.

CHAPTER SEVENTEEN

he moment Beryl was on his family's lands, he exhaled. The moment he ushered her inside the castle's stone walls, his shoulders relaxed. He did not let Poppy go until she was behind the locked door of his room.

"Come," he said to her, beckoning his mate to the washroom. "I want to clean you of that lion's scent."

She cringed. Her features had contorted into the same look of discomfort from back in the forest when he'd raised his voice at her. He had regrets that he'd frightened her, but she needed to understand the gravity of the situation. He'd almost lost her to the lions. Just a few more moments and Ari would've been within his rights to scoop her into his paws and run back to his den with Beryl's treasure.

Just that thought had his dragon baring its incisors. It would not come to pass. Poppy was now and would forever be his mate. No lion would ever touch her. No lion would ever see her in all of her glory.

She stood in her garb; a cloth shirt that molded to her curvy form and tight pants that showed off her assets. Her arms were crossed self-consciously over her body. He would never understand her. She was the most beautiful creature he'd ever seen, and yet she constantly ducked her head and twisted her body as though that fact were not true.

After a moment, Poppy moved toward him. Beryl stretched out his hands, but he didn't disrobe her. He wanted her permission. Not that he needed it. She was his to protect. However, he did want her trust.

"It's my job as your mate to care for you," he said. "Let me."

There was command in his voice, but also a plea. Poppy's gaze lifted as her hands lowered from her chest. She placed her hands in his.

Inside, Beryl felt something uncoil. He'd handed over his soul when he'd received her. Now, she was unlocking his heart.

He slipped her top off. Her breath trembled as he

did so. Her hands didn't go to shield her breasts. She was trying to cover her scales.

Beryl kissed the backs of her fingers. He nuzzled his nose against her digits, pushing them aside until he got at the skin she tried to hide.

Pressing his lips to the first spot, he said, "You are perfect."

"I'm not," she insisted, her voice shaky. "I'm scarred."

"I've told you already. These aren't scars. They're scales. It means you were made for me."

Beryl tugged the tight pants she wore down her body, pulling off her shoes before he stood. He stepped back to look at the wonder of his mate. Poppy was soft curves and dips with a smattering of dark scales along her arms and legs.

Poppy moved to cover herself again.

"Hands," he commanded. He was tired of fighting his mate for this part of her. "You are mine. Do not cover what is mine."

He'd raised his voice again. Poppy inhaled sharply, her eyes going wide. But not with fear. She was trembling now. The scent that hit his nose told him that she was in need.

Beryl lifted her into the tub of hot, soapy water. Then he disrobed under her watchful gaze. He liked that his form pleased his mate's eyes. He knew his muscles and physique was what females enjoyed gazing upon. From now on, each bench press, each bicep curl, each upright row was only for his mate's enjoyment.

His dragon was sedate as he climbed in the tub behind Poppy. He pulled her bare body back to him and rested the back of her head against his chest. Poppy fit him like a puzzle piece, like they had been made for each other. Had it only been a day since she'd come into his life?

Poppy reached for the washcloth, but he took it from her hand.

"Don't you want me to wash you?" she asked.

"It's the male who tends to his female."

"That's not the way it works in my world."

"The men of your world are weak," Beryl snorted. "It's women who make men strong. That's why we grow muscles, so that we are strong enough to protect our treasures."

Beryl dipped the cloth into the water. He squeezed it of excess water. Then he ran it in careful circles over Poppy's chest.

"I'm not sure how I'll make you strong," she said, "when I've been weak my whole life."

She was silent for a while as he washed her. He

let her have the quiet as he massaged the suds into her body, erasing any trace of lion fuzz.

"Where I come from, little girls aren't treasured," Poppy said after a while. "They're not always protected. My mother used her body to make money. One of her clients used to look at me funny. Then one night after he was finished with her and she was asleep, he came to my bedroom."

The cloth slipped from Beryl's fingers. His hold on his mate tightened.

"He started touching me. I was too scared to call for help. I didn't want to make him angry. Even as a child, I knew we needed the money. So, I just lay there and let him."

The water had grown tepid as they both sat in its depths. It began to boil as the dragon roused. "Did he—"

"He didn't. My mom came into the room. She hit him over the head and knocked him out before he could ..."

Thank the Goddess, her mother was there. Beryl had always known that a mother's highest calling was protecting their young. That's why the guilt had clawed at him all his life.

"Where is your mother now?" he asked.

"The man who tried to hurt me died, and my mom went to jail for his murder."

"Jail? She was caged for protecting you?"

"He was an important man, so she got into trouble. That's the way it works where I'm from. She died in jail." Poppy turned her body, curling into his chest. Her hand rested on one of his pecs, and she gazed down at the spot on her forearm. "She had the same skin condition as me. She had fire in her blood."

"Dragons and halflings aren't meant for that world. I'm sorry she didn't survive. But I will honor her bravery and her sacrifice for you."

Poppy tilted her head up to meet his gaze. The scent of desire permeated the waters of the tub. The room filled with steam with his dragon near the surface.

"Are you still going to punish me?" she asked.

"I'm afraid I must," he said. "You need to learn your lesson."

He reached down into the water for her waist. When both hands were filled with her curves, he lifted her to stand over him. Beryl rested his head back against the side of the basin and positioned Poppy's hips over his.

"You ready?" he asked.

There was desire mixed with confusion in her eyes.

"I'm going to lick your treasure spot. You're going to stand there and take it. If you dare to tell me to stop, I'll lick you for five minutes longer. Do you understand me?"

"I ... oh ..."

Beryl sealed his mouth around her soft flesh. With only his second pull, her knees were already knocking against his ears. He showed some mercy and cupped her ass, but he used his position to push her up and down on his tongue.

The top half of her body was already bent over. She gripped the edge of the tub. She was so responsive to his touch like she'd never received such pleasure before.

She was his. His perfect mate. So soft. So sensitive. So reactive to his every move.

He cursed Ari that he would now have to wait to claim her properly. He knew that breaking that particular rule amounted to forfeit. This was one battle he'd die before losing. There were no rules against tasting her, pleasing her, letting her know whom she belonged to.

Poppy learned her lesson that night. She didn't once beg him to stop. She took every ounce of pleasure Beryl gave her. Standing over him while they were in the tub. Bent over the chair next to the bed. Lying flat on her back on the bed.

Beryl kept his head between his mate's legs until she went limp, finally passing out from all the pleasure. After all the fights he'd been in, after all the bouts he'd won, he never felt as victorious as looking down at his contented mate as she slept in his arms.

In the morning, he would start training for war. The lions had no idea what they awakened inside of him. Beryl's dragon was no longer on a mindless rampage. Man and beast were focused on the prize, and they would gut anything and anyone who stood in their way.

CHAPTER EIGHTEEN

Rolling over in the large bed, Poppy's thighs were sore. Like she'd run a marathon. Up twenty-six flights of stairs.

She'd often hurt after sex with Bruce. He was not a gentle lover. But this was the good kind of sore.

The muscles of her inner legs throbbed as she sat up. Her lips were swollen and sensitive to the touch. Even her wrists ached from when her dragon held her down after her fifth orgasm when she was sure she couldn't take anymore. She'd been wrong. And then wrong again.

Poppy looked around for Beryl. He'd held her the whole night. But now he was nowhere to be found.

She told herself not to panic. Beryl wasn't Bruce. Bruce fucked her, but he never slept with her. He preferred the couch, or better yet, some other woman's bed. One of his tricks who knew how to give pleasure back to him. That wasn't Poppy.

Before last night, she'd never taken any pleasure from sex. Come to think of it, Beryl hadn't taken any pleasure from her. She knew what a man's orgasm looked like. She knew what it felt like inside of her. She knew what a mess it made afterward when she had to clean the evidence from her person.

Beryl hadn't gotten that look. He hadn't spilled anything inside her or on her. He hadn't even taken his clothes off. Come to think of it, she hadn't seen anything but his chest since her first night in his bed.

Poppy got up from the bed. She pulled clothes over her head and up her legs. All the while, she tried not to jump to conclusions.

She'd probably slept late. Beryl might be an early bird. She knew he worked in the mines. He was probably there ... and not in some other woman's bed.

That was it. He had work to do. She couldn't expect him to hang out with her all day.

Perhaps, she could work with him? She had no

intentions of simply sitting around all day. That's what she'd done all her life; hidden inside because of her scars.

No. Not scars. Scales.

She had the blood of a dragon inside her veins. She was made of strong stuff. Those spots on her body were nothing to hide from anymore.

Beryl wasn't ashamed of her. He reveled in how she looked. Poppy hadn't missed how he'd lit up when she stood before him naked. The man wasn't faking it. He liked what he saw.

Looking in the mirror now, she couldn't help but smile. She brushed a hand over the starburst pattern on her shoulder, the one Beryl couldn't stop kissing. She pushed up her sleeves so that her scales could be seen.

Poppy headed out of their room and immediately got lost in the maze of the castle. Each door looked the same. Each turn she took only served in turning her around. Turning down one hall, she heard voices. She followed the sounds to another nondescript door. But the scene inside brought her up short.

Chryssie and Cardi were both propped up on a massive bed. Cardi lay at the bottom, her legs bent at the knees, her heels bouncing downwards toward her Jordache covered rear. Chryssie lay at the top of the bed, her hand resting on the small bump on her belly.

On the other side of the bed sat Elek. The quiet dragon shifter had his arm wrapped loosely around the shoulders of an elderly woman. The woman was dressed in the nightclothes of someone out of the Victorian age. White frilly cap, high necked nightgown that reached down to her wrists. All four of them stared at a television screen.

On the screen, colorful puppets danced around. Their shaggy hair flew out from their heads as they sang. Their puppeteer hands clapped in time to the beat.

"Hey, Poppy," called Chryssie. "Come join us. Did you watch *Fraggle Rock* as a kid?"

"Um, no," said Poppy. The kid's show debuted on HBO, and her mom could never afford cable. She knew the show dealt with deeper issues than sharing and caring like the normal cartoons. It would slip into the arena of spirituality, racial and social identity, and environmental issues. So, no, it did not make the after school cartoon line up or PBS Kids.

"Hi, Cardi. Good morning, Elek. Hello, ma'am."

Cardi wiggled her toes, not turning her face from the television. Elek gave her a slight nod of his head, also not taking his gaze off the TV. The woman didn't even blink. She gave absolutely no indication that she was aware of Poppy's presence.

"Poppy, this is Miya," said Cardi. "Miya, this is Poppy. She belongs to Beryl. Can you believe it? Beryl got himself a sacrifice."

Cardi rolled over so that her head was resting on Miya's covered legs. As she flipped her body, Cardi's gaze never left the screen. Miya blinked once.

"Miya is Elek's mom," said Chryssie. "But we've all kind of adopted her. Dragon births are hard on women. Most don't survive, but Miya did because she's strong." Chryssie patted Miya's shoulder with one hand, while the other caressed her belly.

Miya blinked. But her eyes didn't reopen. Poppy's gaze darted to her chest. It still rose and fell. Hopefully, that meant she was just sleeping.

"So," said Cardi, finally breaking her gaze from the TV. "You and Beryl ..."

"Cardi, that's inappropriate," said Chryssie.

"How's it inappropriate when we could all hear them boinking last night?"

Poppy's face heated so thoroughly she thought her eyes glazed over in red. She didn't want to correct Cardi on the boinking bit since that technically didn't happen.

"It's good for me to know," said Cardi. "Corun can throw down. Beryl can throw down. Hopefully, if ever Kimber grows a pair and boinks me, I'll find out he can throw down as well."

"Kimber has a pair," said Elek.

"Huh," huffed Cardi, snuggling up to rest her head on Miya's bosom. "I'm glad he's shown them to you because he sure as heck hasn't shown me."

"He will," said Elek. "When you're ripe."

"When will that be? I'm sure I'm already eighteen. I think I might be nineteen." Cardi turned back to Poppy. "Time runs weird on this side of the Veil. Miya here was born in the 1800s. I think it's like a year here for each decade back on the other side."

"If so," said Chryssie, "then that would make you twenty, maybe closer to twenty-one."

Cardi sat bolt up. "Twenty-one? Are you kidding me? I'm not only legal, but I'm of legal drinking age? This changes everything."

Cardi crawled off the bed and headed out the door. Chryssie shook her head.

"Is she off to boink Kimber?" Poppy asked.

"I doubt it," said Chryssie. "She's probably going to raid the liquor cabinet."

The two women giggled. Elek shushed them, pointing to the television set where the fraggles had begun another song and dance routine about accepting each other's differences.

Poppy lowered her voice. "I was trying to find Beryl. I thought he might be in the mines."

"He's out in the back training for the fight."

Poppy had forgotten about the fight. She didn't like the thought of Beryl fighting those massive lions. "Would you mind showing me where?"

"I'll take you." Chryssie kissed Mom.

The older woman's eyes opened and focused back on the television screen.

"What's wrong with her?" asked Poppy when they were out of the room.

"Unlike us, she doesn't have fire in her blood. Many sacrifices died after giving birth. Corun and Kimber's mother lived a few days and died. The triplets—Beryl, Ilia, and Rhoyl's mom—barely made it to the end of her pregnancy. They had to cut the babies out."

Poppy felt sick at Chryssie's words. Looking down at the small bump on her belly, Poppy swallowed. She wouldn't ask. But it looked like Chryssie anticipated the question.

"It was a gruesome existence being a sacrifice,"

said Chryssie. "But things are different now. You, me, Cardi, we're part dragon. So, we'll survive."

Poppy wasn't even sure if she wanted children. But she also knew she wouldn't deny Beryl if he told her it was what he wanted. She would give him everything, anything. Wasn't' that what love was?

It had to be. Because she knew with certainty that she loved Beryl. Enough to die for him if it were necessary.

"Look, there he is," said Chryssie. "I'm going to head to my room to lay down for a bit. See you later, okay?"

Poppy nodded as Chryssie turned to go, or at least she thought she did. They had come out to the back of the castle. Many pieces of equipment she'd seen in the workout room had been brought outside in the crisp day. Beryl was rhythmically hitting a boxing bag hanging from a tree. His shirt was off, his muscles gleaming under the sun. He looked magnificent.

Watching him, Poppy was brought back to the other night when he'd rocked her body with pleasure. How did hands like meat cleavers deliver such bliss? How did a mouth, cruel with concentration, make her shiver with complete satisfaction?

"Is he just as powerful in bed?"

"Even more so. I thought he'd tear my petals off."

Seated on the grass were three fairies. They were each breathtakingly beautiful with full lashes, pastel skin, and long limbs. On top of that, they each smelled like honey on a stick.

"Beryl always wants sex after a fight. I've had him three times now."

"He likes it after working out, too. I've had him five times."

"I'd like to have him at least once before he's off the market."

"Off the market? Oh, you mean because of the human? If he wanted to claim her, he would've already had sex with her."

"She's right. What virile shifter can withstand a human sacrifice? There must be something wrong with her. I wouldn't be surprised if Beryl threw the fight and let the lions have her."

"Great, then we could have more of him. I bet he'll take all three of us at once when he's done with his workout."

The saccharine in the air turned Poppy's stomach. Her worst fears had been right. Beryl didn't want her sexually. Not only that, he would be getting it from other women, and right here under her nose.

Poppy hadn't escaped her past at all. It had followed her here. She was just as undesirable as she'd been on earth. Only this time, it actually hurt because she was in love with the man who didn't want her.

CHAPTER NINETEEN

The fight was gathering more attention than he'd anticipated. Previously, Beryl would've loved the hype. He would've welcomed the rigor of training. But all he wanted to do was get back to his mate.

He couldn't wait for the sun to set so that he could climb into their bed and burrow between her thighs. It was now his favorite place in the world, the only place he wanted to be.

He was happy to only use his tongue and his fingers for now. Maybe even forever. Getting Poppy pregnant wasn't a goal. The Valkyrie said that Chryssie, Cardi, and Poppy would survive because they had fire in their blood. But Beryl didn't care to chance it.

He'd already murdered one woman. He'd been the first to claw his way out of his mother's belly. He could remember the sound of her heartbeat. And then, after he'd drawn his first breath, the rhythmic beating that had put him to sleep every night had stopped.

Beryl knew the sound of Poppy's heartbeat. He'd awakened to the feel of her pulse in his hands as he'd held her wrapped in his arms. He'd tasted the breath of life on her lips. He would not allow any harm to come to her. He'd promised. Not only her, but he'd also promised himself.

His beast was in turmoil. He wanted his mate, but he was terrified of what he might accidentally do to her.

"Need a break, Great Hulk?"

Beryl frowned at the sound of the familiar voice. He turned to find Aster rising from a seated position in the grass. Her purple skin gleamed in the sunlight. What was she doing here?

"I seem to have come down with a case of Berylmania." The wanton fairy sauntered over to him. "I was hoping you might have the cure."

Beryl watched her lithe body swaying in the breeze. How had he ever found pleasure in something so slight? He knew how. He'd been in a desert with no poppies around. Upstairs was an oasis. So, why was he standing down here?

Beryl opened his mouth to turn the fairy down. Before he could, his nose caught something sweet-smelling. A scent that far surpassed the saccharine of the fairies.

Poppy.

She was backing away from the door. Her head was down, but he could see something coming from her eyes. Were those tears?

He was torn. He wanted to find who hurt her and rip them to shreds. But he also wanted to gather her in his arms and comfort her. The need to comfort her won out.

"Poppy?"

She startled, coming to a standstill when he caught up to her in the doorway.

Beryl turned her to face him. "What's wrong?"

"Nothing, I'm fine."

The world tinged green with those words. He gripped her shoulders. "Do not lie to me."

She shut her eyes and winced. Beryl froze. All around, everyone in the yard stopped what they were doing to look over at him. He saw it on the flowers' faces.

Brute. Beast. Hulk.

But worse, he saw it on his mate's closed eyelids which were scrunched tight. In her tensed shoulders. In her small breaths. She was waiting for him to strike out. At least this time she didn't raise her hands. That's what broke him.

His mate would've taken the assault if he had decided to dole it out to her. He knew he needed to let her go, but he couldn't. Not yet. First, he needed to get them away from prying eyes. He didn't care what anyone else thought about him besides her.

Beryl swept Poppy inside. She closed her eyes and rested her head on his shoulder. Her tears dried up, and her breathing calmed. He was not gratified. It was clear she was still ready to receive her punishment.

Punishments must mean something very different on the other side of the Veil. Here, when a male punished a female, it was only to take away her say in her pleasure. Not to take away any actual pleasure.

It would appear human males inflicted actual pain on their females. That was something Beryl would never understand. He'd accidentally hurt his mother, and that shame would stay with him for the rest of his life.

Climbing to their room, Beryl sat Poppy down at

the edge of the bed. She scooted back slowly. When she reached the headboard, she lay back and spread her thighs. She turned her head to the side and lay still.

Beryl felt sick to his stomach as he watched her submit in this manner. Forget the fight with Ari, he would be traveling to Valhalla to find the bastard who had abused her. He'd steal him away and use his head as a punching back.

"Sit up." He'd meant it as a gentle request, but it came out as a growled command.

Poppy did as she was told. She still wouldn't meet his gaze.

"You tell me you're fine when clearly, you're not." Beryl took a deep breath to calm himself and the dragon down. "It breaks me when you lie to me. I crave your trust."

His words must have sparked something in her, because she turned to him, her eyes flashing. "You want my trust when you've invited other women over to take care of your needs?"

Beryl opened his mouth. Then closed it. Then tried again. "What?"

Poppy bit her lip, seeming as surprised as he was at the words that came out of her mouth. But then she opened her mouth and continued, raising her chin a little higher. "You tell me I can't go anywhere. You leave me alone to go and do your work. Now you're bringing other women around me to fuck."

"Other women? To fuck?" How could she think such a thing? He'd cut off his dick before he put it anywhere near another woman. How did she not see that? He needed to make her see.

Beryl lunged for her, needing her close so that she could understand the depth of his feelings for her. He grabbed her arms, and she gasped. She shut her eyes and turned her cheek, tense once more. Regret on her brow. Fear in the flare of her nostrils.

"I am a monster," he breathed as he released her.

He sank to his knees, his head low. He'd never been in a position of supplication before. But this felt right, to kneel before his treasure and beg her forgiveness.

"It's hard for me to be gentle with you," he said. "I'm still learning how. And when you lie to me, it drives me crazy. When you say things that make no sense, like me wanting anyone but you, I don't know what to do?"

Poppy looked as startled and uncertain as he did.

"I'm supposed to know what to do, and I don't," he said. "I'm so terrified of hurting you because I'm stronger. If I don't hurt you physically, I hurt you in some other way."

"It's fi—"

"Don't." He held a finger to her mouth. "Don't say fine. It's a lie. Tell me the truth."

Poppy pursed her lips together. She chewed at her lower lip as though she didn't know what to say.

"You have to understand that when you hurt, I hurt. I'm used to being strong. I don't know how to handle weakness. I would do anything for you. But I need to know what hurt you so that I can crush it. Even if it's me."

"I don't want you to touch any other women," she said finally.

"I haven't," he said. "I wouldn't. You are it for me. I'll never want another woman now that I have you."

"What about those fairies?"

"Fairies?" He'd forgotten about Aster and the other fairies that had been watching him work out. He hadn't even noticed them until Aster approached him. "They are my past. Would you like me to tell them to leave?"

"I ..."

He let her go and marched back out the door, but Poppy caught his arm. "I don't want you anywhere near them."

"Fine," he said. "I'll never talk to another fairy. Will this please you?"

She searched his gaze. Beryl wished he could open his eyes wider so that she could see straight into his heart. Finally, she nodded, but the bob of her head was still a bit uncertain.

"What else can I do to please you?" he asked.

"You can take me to bed."

"Done." He scooped her into his arms and headed to the bed. This was what he'd wanted all along, to put his face back between her thighs.

"And you can have sex with me," she said. "The real kind."

His steps faltered. When he looked down at her, her face crumbled.

"I knew it," she said. "You don't want me."

"Don't want you?" he repeated. Was that what she thought? "I want you. I want you more than anything in the world. But if I claim you, if I penetrate you, I would forfeit Ari's challenge. By right, he could claim you."

"He doesn't have to know. I wouldn't tell. Sex is what I need to know that you want me."

Beryl took a deep breath. All that filled his nostrils was Poppy's sweet arousal. It fogged his brain and hardened his dick.

"We can't." That was the right answer. So, why did it feel so wrong?

"It's because I'm not good in bed, isn't it? But I can learn. I will learn. I'll do whatever you tell me."

Beryl sat Poppy down on the bed. Then he took a few steps away from her. Those words had riled his dragon up. The beast was straining inside his gut. If he got out, he would happily attack Poppy.

Beryl couldn't let that happen. What if she got hurt? No, there was no what if. He'd definitely hurt her.

"All I know how to do is lay there," Poppy said.

She pulled her legs up under her. She looked miserable. His dragon wanted to reach up and punch him in the face.

"I don't know how to move or any tricks. I can't even give a decent blow job. But I've never really tried hard. I'd try hard with you."

It was too much. He had his dragon roaring in his ears. His pants were too tight. The smell of her arousal was thick in the air. It was three against one. Four, if he counted Poppy making her pleas. That's when Beryl realized this would be the first fight that he would lose.

CHAPTER TWENTY

There it was, written all over his face; hesitancy. What man hesitated when a woman offered up her body for sex. One that didn't want her, that's who. Those fairies were right. There must be something wrong with her.

She turned away from Beryl, needing to put distance between herself and the man who was now stuck with her. Maybe it would be best if the lions won her. Since there was no way she could win the man she wanted.

"Poppy, I haven't had sex with you because I'm afraid of hurting you."

She paused, running his words over and over again in her mind. Nope. They didn't make any sense no matter how she reordered them.

"You're so small. You're human with flesh and bones. What if I break you?"

Poppy turned back and stared up at the big, strong man before her. "You haven't had sex with me because you're afraid of hurting me?" The words sounded ridiculous as they came out of her mouth, but Beryl nodded.

"Look at me, Poppy." He lifted his arms and held out his hands. "I could crush you with a flick of my wrist."

"But you wouldn't." It wasn't a question. She knew it to be true.

Beryl confirmed by shaking his head. A look of anguish washed over his handsome features. "You have no idea how much I want you."

"You want me?"

"Of course, I do. Since the first second I laid eyes on you, I've wanted you."

"To soothe your beast?"

"I thought I needed to claim you to gain control over my dragon. But that wasn't the whole thing. Taking care of you, providing for you, protecting you, that's what has brought me balance. I don't need sex to be in control. I just need you to be with me. You are my center."

Words left her. Along with her breath. Along with her balance.

Poppy lost her center of gravity at the sound of Beryl's words. What was up was down. What was left was right. What was wrong was now solved.

Beryl's arms came around her. "I think this is what they call love."

She'd never thought she'd have love returned to her. A girl like her, born from a prostitute in a trailer park. Poppy had been used all her life. She'd taken hits and kicks and insults just to survive. But today, she had become the center of someone else's life.

Beryl didn't want to use her for her body. He didn't want her services on her knees in any manner. He didn't use words to hurt her or put her in her place. He was afraid to touch her because he thought he might cause physical harm.

"I don't want anyone else but you," Beryl continued. "No fairy, no other woman, not even my own hand. I want you to never feel obligated to lay with me. You might be the sacrifice, but I would do anything for you."

"Anything?"

"Name it."

"I want you to claim me."

He sucked down a breath. With that inhale, he

seemed to grow bigger before her eyes. His chest inflated. His hands balled into fists. Poppy was pretty certain his pants fit tighter.

He looked to her like Bruce Banner transforming into the Incredible Hulk. Would he bust out of those pants? Oh, please do.

"Actually," she said. "I take that back. I want to claim you."

Now, it was Beryl taking a step back from her. As he did, his eyes changed from brown to emerald. The dragon was near the surface. It was clear to see that the beast inside of him liked that prospect.

"I thought I was a victim after all I've been through," she said.

Poppy stepped forward. She came toe to toe with Beryl. Her head only reached up to his chest. She put a hand there. His heart pounded at the touch of her palm.

"Now, I see that I survived everything in my life to get this prize. To get to you." She wrapped both of her hands around him. He was too large for her fingers to meet at the back, so she rested them on his ass. "I claim you, Beryl. And I'm getting my booty right now."

He cracked a smile, and that's when she knew she had him.

"Take me to bed," she demanded.

The hesitation on his face lasted for less than a fraction of a millisecond. Then she was in his arms. Everything blurred and before she blinked they were on the bed.

He was on top of her, but his body didn't touch hers. She'd deal with his fear of crushing her later. Poppy's first order of business was getting her man naked. Men lost the ability to reason when they were naked.

She tugged at the ties on his shorts. They gave easily. She pushed them down his thighs, revealing muscle after muscle.

She did gasp at the size of his manhood. Her Beryl was a big boy, indeed. But she did not doubt that he would fit inside of her. She was made for him.

Poppy pulled off her clothes from within the cage of his arms. His long, thick penis brushed her belly as she slipped off the clothes she'd been wearing. Beryl watched her, his body still hovering over hers. His face was a mix of desire and agony.

"Lie on your back," Poppy said.

Beryl did as she asked. His large body crashed down beside her. He let out a long, harsh breath as if he'd just finished the hardest workout of his life. And they hadn't even started yet.

Poppy climbed on top of him. Her sexy beast sprawled his large form on the bed. He put his hands behind his head and held onto the bars of the bed. His gaze lingered on her spots more than they did on her breasts.

She brought her core over the head of his eager penis. Foreplay was not on the menu tonight.

"Poppy wait," he said. "You're not ready."

"I've been ready for you since that first night." The evidence was pooling between her thighs as she aimed the head of his cock at her entrance.

She began her descent down onto him. They both gasped at the breach of her skin. The stretch was real, but it wasn't painful. Not really. Especially not with how much she wanted him, wanted this.

For his part, Beryl held still. His eyes glowed bright green, but there was brown at the center. Man and dragon were one at this moment.

"You are my life," he said on a sigh of utter contentment. "My every moment, my every breath, will be in service to you."

That made her falter. She would never get used to his compliments, his devotion, his love. Her eyes pooled with tears. Beryl released the metal headboard and wrapped her in his arms. Gently, he kissed the tears away. As she relaxed into his embrace, she slid down onto him until she was fully seated on his lap.

She'd been right. He hadn't hurt her. He'd filled her with more kindness and strength than she'd ever imagined possible.

Poppy lifted her hips until he was nearly out of her. Slowly, she slid down his length. For his part, Beryl supported her weight. His lips rested over hers, not kissing, just sharing her breath.

She rode him carefully, unhurriedly, deeply. She had to. He was a big boy, after all. Too fast and she could very well hurt herself.

The truth of the matter was that she did break apart. Her orgasm crept up on her. When it hit, her clenching muscles were stretched so far, her channel so full, that her entire body shook with the force of it.

Beryl threw his head back and let out a guttural roar. The last millimeter of space inside Poppy was filled with this warm seed. They remained like that, stuck together without a breath of room between them.

"Now you're mine," she said.

A low rumble of approval sounded in his chest.

orning crept over his mate's face like a kiss. Illuminating her cheek. Glossing over her lips. Shimmering on her forehead. Beryl frowned at the sun's rays. He was jealous even of its heat caressing her.

Last night had been beyond anything he could've imagined. Watching Poppy over him, claiming him, it was the sexiest thing in the world. His cock got hard and eager just thinking about it. But he took deep breaths to get it under control.

Yes, they had fit together. Though it had been a snug fit. He was sure she would be feeling it this morning.

He had been a randy beast all his adult life. He wanted more of his mate right now, but he would wait to take her again. He would wait forever if he needed. Just so long as he got to hold her in his arms, to keep her safe, and warm, and fed.

Goddess, he'd need to feed her soon. There was a good chance she was carrying his hatchlings. That thought lowered his morning tent.

What if Poppy was pregnant? What if they were triplets? He knew there was fire in her blood, but birthing dragons was still a dangerous business whether the woman be human or halfling.

He'd torn his mother apart on his entrance into the world. Even before he was out, inside of her, he had hoarded all the sustenance, weakening his two other brothers. What if he put even one such beast inside of her?

Beryl rose from the bed. He went out on the balcony into the dawning sun. Poppy may have given him balance in his life, but he still was unsteady about his past.

He spotted Rhoyl sleeping beneath a tree in dragon form. He could barely remember what his brother looked like in human form. He might never see that again. Would likely never see the man again. Was that his fault too?

Down below, Ilia opened the back door, letting out the two fairies Beryl had sent away the other day.

Ilia was always getting Beryl's scraps. His human form was scrawny because Beryl was either taking from him or putting a fist in his mouth.

Yet here Beryl was, the biggest of the three. With a mate who had put his world back on its axis. Life wasn't fair.

"Hey."

Warm arms came around him followed by that enticing scent that belonged only to her.

"I was worried for a second," she said. "I thought you'd left me again."

"Never." He pulled her into his arms, clutching her tight. His worries about being too rough with her, too ardent, were cooled. But he still was careful with her.

"No, I know," she said. "I just have to get used to this new life. I have to get used to being with someone who loves me, someone who wants to take care of me. I'm still learning how to do that for myself."

Beryl nuzzled her neck. He dragged his lips over the claiming mark he'd put there. Then he nipped at the sensitive spot he'd found behind her ear.

"I blamed myself for all the bad stuff in my life," Poppy continued. "I told myself I was choosing to be where I was, to stay in an abusive relationship.

Part of that was true. But you know what I realized?"

Beryl was listening. But it was best he kiss the space between her brows than give his full attention to her words. Otherwise, he'd be flying to Valhalla to rip apart the man who'd hurt her.

"I realized that I need to forgive myself. The same way that I found the strength to claim my new life and my new love, I need to deal with my past and forgive myself. I'm going to do that. You helped show me that."

"Me?" He leaned back so that he could see her face. "I did?"

"Of course." She grinned. "I wouldn't be this strong if it hadn't been for you. I wouldn't have known that I could if you didn't show me."

Beryl looked at the woman he loved. She had come to him small and weak. Last night, she'd stood up for herself. She'd demanded what she wanted. And, even though he'd had his doubts, she had been the one to claim him.

"Finding my strength brought me to a conclusion." Poppy took a deep breath. "I want to have your babies."

For the second time this morning, his erection went limp.

"I never wanted to bring kids into this world before," she said. "But we're not in my old world. This is my new life, where I'm in control. I just claimed myself a dragon."

Beryl clasped his hand behind her neck and brought her forehead to his lips. "Yes, you did. You claimed me, and I'm yours."

"And babies?"

His dragon reared up, loving that idea. That was one of its priorities in life; to procreate. He had to remind himself that Poppy wasn't his mother. His mother had been human. Poppy had fire in her blood. She should survive.

It was the *should* that gave him pause. Chryssie was only a couple of months pregnant. But each day her belly grew large.

They had the technology now where they could see the babies. Corun had bartered with Morrigan to bring back something called an ultrasound. It allowed him to see in Chryssie's belly, although it didn't make any sounds. They could do the same if Poppy became pregnant, to make sure she was safe. But not yet.

"I want you all to myself for a while," he said finally.

She sighed, pushing out a pouty lip. But she

didn't argue. That was one problem solved. But another still loomed.

"What are we going to do today?" she asked. "Do you have to mine? Is there something I can do to help? Or maybe we could go back to bed?"

"I have to train."

"Train? Why? Oh, wait, don't tell me. You're still going to fight the lions."

"Of course, I am. I made a covenant. We take those seriously here in the Veil. They'll come after you if I don't. If they find out I've claimed you, it would be a forfeit."

"But I already made my choice. I claimed you."

"It doesn't work that way. It does between us. But not between males."

She scowled. "This is ridiculous. I break free from the misogyny of one realm and land smack dab in the center of another."

"I won't lose you," Beryl insisted. "I'll rip Ari's head off before it comes to that."

Poppy didn't respond.

Was that too violent for her? Had he scared her again? He could be gentle with her, but anything that threatened her would lose a limb at best, life at worst.

"I didn't mean to scare you," he said into her hair.

"I'm not scared of you." She looked up at him.

She wasn't. He felt her relax entirely within his hold. Beryl wrapped his arms around her and squeezed. It would've been a submission hold, but he was the one who had submitted to her will.

"You are my champion," she said. "You are my Professor Hulk."

"What's that?"

"It's when Hulk and Bannon merge into one in *Endgame*."

Endgame? Was that a new season of *The Incredible Hulk* that he hadn't seen? Whatever it was, he liked the sound of it; a smart Hulk. One who thought before he smashed.

"I feel safe for the first time in my life," she said. "I know that no one and nothing will ever hurt me again. But I don't want you to get hurt."

"He will not win."

She pinched her lips together and clenched her jaw. Beryl couldn't help himself. He captured her puckered lips with his own.

He bit and suckled and nibbled at her until she softened. Her arms went around his neck. Her body pressed into his until he felt the sharp points of her nipples.

It took everything in him to pull away. "I'll let you take out your frustration on me. But later."

Once again, she didn't answer. Her pliable lips tightened into another frown. Goddess, she was adorable when she was mad. He would come back and kiss that look off her face. And then kiss her somewhere else to get a different look on her face.

CHAPTER TWENTY-TWO

oppy pulled on a pair of jeans and felt like she was mostly naked. There were a lot of rips in them like something out of a metal band music video. On the plus side, they showed off her scales.

Wow. When had showing off her spots become a plus side? Probably the moment she realized her mate couldn't stop caressing and kissing them.

So, yeah. She wanted to keep her best assets visible even though she wasn't off to see Beryl right now.

Maybe it was the sex juices flowing through her lady bits? Maybe it was her newfound sense of confidence after riding Beryl? In any case, Poppy was determined to be the captain of her ship of her life from now on. And that included ending this stupid claiming fight over her.

She'd already staked her claim. She wasn't letting anyone else stake her again without her complete consent. And that would include Beryl if he tried to stop her from her errand.

Which was why she was sneaking out.

Poppy knew her overprotective mate wouldn't hesitate to chain her to the bed. Which she might have trouble protesting because she knew what he was capable of with a little bit of gold chain.

Slinking around the corner, she met with another overprotective male. Elek materialized from the shadows. The two stared at each other. Elek's gaze narrowed, his pupils dilating. Poppy held her tongue, but she got the sense he knew her exact intentions.

He pointed her toward the door. "Keep to the forest. And remember, it takes courage to stand up and speak up. But sitting and listening take strength, too."

With those puzzling words, he disappeared back into the shadows.

Okay. Riddles weren't her thing. But it was cool that she had one ally. And if anything went wrong, someone would know where she went.

Not that she thought anything would go wrong. She'd found her voice. She'd use it now when she spoke to the lioness.

"Stop."

Poppy yelped, her hand fluttered to her heart.

Cardi doubled over in laughter. Even though she looked grown, the girl behaved like a child. She wore an orange off the shoulder blouse with black bra straps on show and a black mini with leggings. If the girl wasn't Madonna's red-haired twin, then Poppy didn't know what.

"Where you off to after we all just got grounded?" Cardi asked.

"I'm just out for a walk around the grounds."

Heat rose to Poppy's cheeks, belying her nonchalance. As a fellow redhead, Cardi could easily call her bluff.

"Bull shit, you're headed to the lion's den."

"How'd you know?"

"I heard you and Beryl boinking last night."

Poppy lifted her chin.

"Do you know where you're going?"

Poppy lowered her chin.

"Want a tour guide?"

"Why are you helping me?"

"Number two because we're sisters, and we have

to stick together. Number one because it will piss Kimber off, and I love pissing him off."

"Why?"

"It's the only way he pays attention to me. Kinda reverse psychology or something. Anyway, let's go."

The sun was high in the sky when they strolled up to the lion's den. Along the way, Cardi belted out the entire *Like a Virgin* album, coaxing Poppy into singing a few bars of *Get into the Groove*. And an especially blush-worthy rendition of the title track of the album where Cardi pointed out during each chorus section that Poppy was no longer a part of the club.

Despite the performance, Poppy was glad for the company and the guidance. Cardi was right, Poppy would've never found it.

They came toward a bunch of skinny trunk trees with wide, flat tops like open umbrellas full of green leaves. They looked like the trees from *The Lion King*. From one of the travel shows Poppy watched, she knew these were Acacia trees, popular in the Savannah of Africa where lions resided back in her world.

A lion shifter opened the door. It wasn't Ari, The Asshole, the one who'd challenged Beryl. It was the other one. The one who'd hit on Cardi.

"Hey, little sinner." He smiled a toothsome grin.

"Hey, Izem. We're here to see your mama."

"Aw, you didn't come for a play date?" He turned his attention to Poppy. "Finally saw Beryl for the gamma-rayed brute he is, huh?"

"No, he's not a brute. He's kind and gentle and the most patient and thorough lover I've ever had."

"TMI. But okay." Izem turned and beckoned them into the den. It was dimly lit and smelled of turned earth and spicy herbs. Animal heads hung on the walls. Pelts lay across the floor. If she didn't know she was in a predator's lair before, she knew it now.

"Well, that was easier than I expected," said the lioness, materializing from a dark crevice in the wall.

Leona's head cocked to the side, and her gaze swept over both girls. Then it narrowed on Poppy. Once again, Poppy knew what a gazelle felt like the moment it realized it was spotted by one of its predators.

"I'm not here to give myself to your son," said Poppy. "There's this thing back on earth called women's rights."

"I tried to explain it," said Cardi. "They don't get it."

"Human women have no rights here," said Leona. "But it's cute you think this is about you. Even Eve relied on Adam. Unfortunately, I can't pull a rib from one of my cubs and make him a woman. I need a human if my kind are to continue. We are the last of our pride."

"I've made my choice," said Poppy. "I've claimed Beryl as my mate, and I'm not having anyone else."

Poppy looked up to find Ari leaning against the door frame. He was even bigger than she remembered. The bruises on his face making him look even more menacing.

"You say you claimed him?" said Leona.

"Yes."

"In the Biblical sense?"

Poppy gulped, knowing the predator had sunk its teeth into her flank.

"Well, that does change things."

Poppy sighed with relief. It was all working out just as Elek had said. She'd stood up courageously by coming here. But she'd also listened, and now things were working out in her favor for once in her life.

"You broke the covenant," said Leona. "That means Beryl forfeits, and you rightfully belong to my son."

"What? No. I'm my own person. I don't belong to anyone."

"Covenants are sacred in this place. Remember, there was that little story of Adam and Eve and the apple. Those two haven't been back here since."

Ari's predatory grin spread, turning his handsome face cruel.

"Welcome to the family, dear." Leona's massive paws reached out and grabbed Poppy.

"You can't do this," said Cardi. "She's under Kimber's protection."

"So are you, but he hasn't claimed you yet," said Leona. "We'd be happy for you to join the family too."

"Yeah," said Izem. "Real happy."

CHAPTER TWENTY-THREE

Beryl took a deep breath and a step forward. Only to choke and catch his foot mid-step and shuffle back. He'd been doing this dance for the last thirty minutes.

Rhoyl and Ilia were tussling in the yard. Rhoyl only had one gash dripping blood across his right shank. Ilia's left shoulder looked lower than his right. Likely dislocated, not broken. Good, it wasn't a real fight, just play.

Why was it so hard to approach his brothers? Beryl knew what he wanted to say to them. At least he thought he did. He was going to take Poppy's advice and apologize to them. He'd forgiven himself for his part in their birth, and their upbringing, and their current state. He lifted his foot again, only to choke one more time and step back.

"What are you doing?"

Beryl jumped at the sound of Kimber's voice. The male stood in the doorway, watching him with a quizzical look on his stern face.

"Nothing." Beryl kicked at a pebble in the grass.

Kimber stood patiently, watching his younger brother. Though he didn't say a word, his features spoke volumes. Kimber was the only parent Beryl had known. It was the same for all of them. Their father only cared about procreation, not his actual progeny.

It was Kimber who'd tended their scrapes, bruises, and bone breaks. He taught them to mine for their treasure. He made them eat their veggies alongside their raw meat.

"Hey, Kimber. I just want to say, you know, thank you."

"For what?"

"You're a good big brother, that's all."

Kimber arched one brow. "You claimed her, didn't you?"

"Yeah, but that's not why—"

Kimber roared his brothers' names. Beryl grimaced as they came over. Rhoyl licked his hind leg, his mouth came away crimson red. Ilia rolled his shoulder. The bones cracked before snapping back into place.

"I'm going to need you two to pull your full weight from now on in the mines," Kimber began. "We need to get production up. Now with three new mouths to feed and more on the way. Plus, there's the matter of Beryl's upcoming fight."

"Why does the fight matter?" asked Ilia. "It's not as if Beryl will lose. He never loses."

Ilia rubbed at a bruise on his neck that Beryl had given him a few days ago.

"He already lost," said Kimber. "He claimed Poppy last night."

"Yeah," said Ilia. "We heard them."

"*She* claimed *me*." Beryl cringed. He hadn't meant to say that out loud. "Well, she did. She wanted to decide for herself. And she chose me."

"Lucky you," said Ilia, but jealousy dripped from his tone. "You got yourself a good one there."

"You're next," said Beryl.

Ilia shrugged. "If the Valkyries find anymore with fire in their blood. Who knows how long it will be."

"I'll contribute some of my gems," Beryl offered.

"I don't need your hand out," said Ilia.

"It's not a handout," said Beryl. "It's help."

"Why would you help me?" asked Ilia.

Now it was Beryl who shrugged. "I haven't been a good brother. Not to either of you." He lifted his gaze to include Rhoyl. "I thought being the biggest and the strongest was the most important thing. But Poppy showed me that it wasn't. She taught me how to be tender and how powerful that is."

Beryl took a step toward Ilia.

The male put his fists up.

Beryl sighed and opened his arms. "I was only going to hug you."

"Why?" Ilia didn't drop his guard.

"I'm trying to apologize and be an evolved man."

"I've been evolved all my life," said Ilia. "Way before you."

"It's not a competition." Beryl's fists clenched in frustration.

Ilia looked skeptical. So did Rhoyl. Hell, so did Kimber.

"All I'm saying is that I've been a beast all of my life. I'm trying to learn to be a better man. And a good man apologizes for his mistakes."

"What mistakes?" asked Kimber.

"The first one," said Beryl. "Killing our mother."

"No." Kimber gripped Beryl's shoulders. "That was not your fault. That is not any of our faults. We each would've saved our mothers if given the chance. And I know for a fact that your mother loved each one of you. I was there."

"I ripped her open," said Beryl.

"Ripped her open? No. She passed away before you each took your first breath. Her body wouldn't give you up. Father ripped each of you out of her before she died."

"He did?" Beryl's eyes flashed emerald. He'd always hated his father, but this new knowledge stoked those flames. "Why did you never tell us this before?"

"I knew." Ilia raised his hand.

"I didn't know that's what you believed," said Kimber.

"Still, I took most of the sustenance in the womb," said Beryl. "Even once out."

"Have any of you lacked for anything in your life?" asked Kimber. "Not enough food? Water? Wine? Shelter? You've had everything. You chose to get stronger. And as you did, you made your brothers stronger."

Beryl wanted to believe his elder brother's words. He just wasn't sure if his younger brothers saw it that way too.

"I knew father ripped her open when I was a

fledgling," said Ilia. "He told me so. Said he considered leaving me inside of her to rot."

"You were clinging to them both," Kimber said to Beryl. "You wouldn't let them go. I know I told you this before."

He had. Only Beryl remembered it differently. He hadn't been holding his brothers back. He'd been trying to bring them forward. All this time, Beryl thought he was the bad guy in the situation.

"Your dragon has always craved to protect something, someone." Kimber rested a strong hand on Beryl's shoulder. "And now you have her."

"Hopefully, he'll keep her," said Ilia. "Unless all this apologizing is a sign of weakness and he can no longer beat Ari."

"Ilia, that's enough," Kimber warned.

One thing that would never change between him and his brothers would be the constant jabs they threw at each other. They might not be huggers, but they certainly weren't pushovers. And just like at the cage matches, like at the bar when Ari had tried to claim Poppy, his brothers would always be there for him. Ready to start or end fights.

"Maybe I can talk to Leona?" said Kimber.

"You'll have to beat Poppy to it," said Elek.

They all turned as Elek materialized from the shadows, munching on an apple.

"She and Cardi left for the lion's den a while ago."

"Why didn't you stop them?" said Kimber.

"Seemed right for women to talk amongst women."

Kimber and Beryl looked at each other. Then they dropped their flesh and took to the skies.

CHAPTER TWENTY-FOUR

"Mama, this isn't fair."

"Life isn't fair, sweet cub." Leona patted Ari on the cheek, but he came away with scratches on his flesh.

She sounded like a concerned mom the way she spoke to Ari, but the tight grip she had on Poppy's arm held tones of Evil Stepmother. Down a long, dark hallway they went. The lions' den was much like the caves where Beryl mined his emeralds. Only these rocks were barren. There were no gems gleaming from their depths.

The first time Poppy had been carted off after her mother was taken, she'd gone along. When Bruce had decided she'd make a good domestic servant, she had been limp too. She'd come to Beryl without protest. But somewhere along the line, she'd grown a backbone. Probably when Beryl had pleasured her so hard that her back bowed.

Orgasms could be lethal if given to the right girl.

Poppy tugged her arm away from Leona. Unfortunately, it didn't do much. Maybe the lioness had been gifted lots of orgasms in her lifetime? She had six children, after all.

Though she was physically weaker than Leona, Poppy's spirit was undaunted. She would not go quietly. She'd finally gained a sense of self. She was not about to give that away to some big-maned brute.

"I won't be docile," said Poppy.

"Good," purred Leona. "I don't want my grand cubs to be born of a weakling. A mother with spirit will ensure they're strong."

"I already had sex with Beryl. I'm probably pregnant with his dragon babies now."

That made her skip a step. Her lip curled, and she flashed her incisors.

"I'll take my chances," said Leona as she pushed Poppy into a room.

"What the-? Boundaries, Mama. We talked about this."

Poppy had thought Izem and Ari were big. The

male scrambling off the bed was so tall he ducked his head a bit so that it didn't hit the ceiling. If he reached his arms out, he might touch both sides of the room. Just one side of his chest was as big as her body.

"I brought you something, Leander. Or rather, someone."

Leander's pants hung low on his hips. There were dark marks all over his fingertips and a few spots around his mouth. He lifted the blanket to hide something beneath the covers. Then he turned to regard Poppy.

Poppy took a step back. Leander's face was set in a permanent grimace. But looking into his eyes, she didn't see the simmering malice that had been in Bruce's or her molester's.

"Why does she smell like Beryl?" said Leander.

"The dragon forfeited the covenant," said Leona.

"Forfeit? You mean he claimed her."

"She is ours now. As eldest, you'll claim her."

Outside the door, Ari mumbled something about the birth canal and big heads.

"I'm not claiming her," said Leander. "She reeks of dragon."

"Hold your nose. Just diddle her with your stick and get her pregnant with cubs."

"Mama—"

"Hurry." Leona had already backed out of the room. The door slammed closed. Followed by the sound of something slamming in front of it.

Leander threw up his hands. When he did, his pants slipped a little lower on his hips, exposing his happy trail. Poppy averted her gaze.

"Oh, sorry about that." He reached for a shirt and shoved his head into it. "And sorry about my mother. She can go overboard when it comes to her cubs."

Leander was not a cub. Neither was Ari or Izem.

Poppy backed into the corner, looking around the room for something to fend him off with.

Leander held up his giant paws. "Hey, hey, calm down, little girl."

"Don't call me little. I'm not a little girl. I'm a grown woman."

"Sorry, that was a bit misogynist of me, wasn't it?"

Poppy didn't respond.

"I'm not gonna hurt you. I'm not sure how you got here, but I know Beryl will come after you and be here at any moment. You want some tea while we wait?"

He walked over to a tea set in the corner of the room. Was this some kind of trick? Was he trying to lure her into a false sense of security and then he'd pounce on her?

"On second thought," he said with the dainty teacup in his hand, "it might be best if we keep to separate sides of the room. When Beryl comes, he'll be looking for blood, and I'm just not up for it tonight. I got a massage from a couple of fairies after our fight the other night, and my muscles are nice and languid."

"That's right," she said. "Beryl is coming for me, and he will kick your ass, so you better stay away."

"Yeah, you're right. Even though this is my mother's fault. But I doubt Beryl will take the time to reason that out." Leander sighed, putting the teacup meant for her on the bed between them. "I really just wanted a quiet night at home."

He picked up his teacup. His pinky went into the air like a proper British gentleman's. His lips pursed as he took a sip and sighed in contentment.

"I'm a pacifist. A lover, not a fighter. But I'm also a mama's boy. I fight to please her. You know how it is with moms."

"My mother is dead. She died in a jail cell after killing the man who touched me when I was a child."

"I'm so sorry." The lion of a man actually looked

sad for her. Then his brows rose to his hairline. "Does Beryl know that?"

Poppy nodded.

"And now you're trapped in a room with me, against your will, after he's mated you. Great, he's going to come here, Hulk out, and totally harsh my vibe. I'm in no mood for Wrestlemania IV."

Poppy had no idea what the giant of a lion-man was talking about. But it sounded like he knew Beryl and what Beryl was capable of. It was clear from how he made himself appear smaller, and his manners that he truly meant Poppy no harm. She decided to trust her gut and label Leander a friend and not foe.

She took a seat on his bed. As she did, a sheet of paper fluttered out. Poppy made out some of the words.

"Don't read that." A low growl came from Leander. The once docile giant turned menacing.

Looks like her bully meter was still getting it wrong.

CHAPTER TWENTY-FIVE

Beryl pumped his legs as he flew. He knew that his legs were ineffectual in the air, but he would do anything necessary to get to her faster.

What had she been thinking going to the lion's den? Hadn't she learned her lesson of going off on her own? He couldn't fathom what her purpose was?

Unless she preferred Ari over him? Although Beryl couldn't see why. The shifter didn't even wrestle or box. He liked karate.

Perhaps Poppy had had her eye on Izem? Izem had an adventurous streak. He was always off in the far reaches of the Veil and spending the night out in the wilderness. Beryl knew Poppy wanted to explore.

Or maybe she'd be interested in Leander.

Leander was almost as big as Beryl. But he knew the lion shifter had a softer side that he only showed those he trusted. Maybe Poppy craved that? Maybe she wanted the cuddly lion over the brute of a dragon.

Deep in his heart, Beryl knew that was wrong. He'd believed her when she'd professed her love for him. Still, there was a part of him that doubted.

The canopy of trees of the lion's territory came into view. He hit the ground running when he reached the lion's den. He'd expected to come face to face with at least two of the cubs outside the entrance. But it was unblocked, completely unguarded. In fact, the door was opened.

Was this a trick?

Kimber was at his side. Along with Ilia. The other three had stayed home to protect Chryssie and her hatchlings.

Beryl kicked the door off its hinges. It was an unnecessary move since it was open and unguarded. But he was so full of aggression, he needed some way to let it out. Professor Hulk went out the door in favor of World War Hulk who would decimate everything in his sight.

She was here. Her heady scent filled the entryway. There were no signs of force anywhere.

Whatever she had come here to do, she'd done it willingly.

Perhaps it was as Elek had said, that Poppy was trying to reason with Leona and get the fight called off now that she was claimed. Unfortunately, Beryl knew things didn't work that way. Especially not with Leona who was still steeped in the old ways.

The lioness would take one sniff of Poppy, smell that she was claimed, and call a forfeit. If Leona brought it to the Valkyries for a decision, they would decide with her. That's why Beryl had to reclaim his mate and then pummel Ari into the ground so that no one would ever challenge him again for Poppy.

She was his. Now and forever.

Voices carried from the den. Beryl knew the way, having been here many times as a fledgling, rough-housing with the cubs. A trill of feminine laughter alongside a deep masculine chuckle came from the inner room. Laughing? Beryl's blood went cold inside his hot veins.

He spied a redhead bent close with a blonde mane. Too close for comfort. This wasn't negotiations. It was flirting.

A roar tore through his throat. The lion turned, eyes glowing yellow-gold looking for the aggressor.

Another pair of eyes flashed him, looking indignant and not the least bit frightened.

"Cardi?" said Beryl.

"Dude, take a chill pill," said Cardi.

Beryl looked around for Poppy. She was nowhere to be seen.

"Cardinal, what are you doing?" said Kimber.

"What does it look like I'm doing? I'm having a private conversation with my friend."

Izem waggled his eyebrows at Kimber, then turned back to Cardi. "You have the most beautiful lips. Has anyone ever told you that?"

"No," Cardi giggled. "Someone has told me that I have the most annoying mouth, but I don't think that is the same."

"Izem," growled Kimber, "move away from her."

Izem looked to Cardi. Cardi glared at Kimber.

"He doesn't have to move anywhere," said Cardi. "He's asked me on a date."

"He did what?" shouted Kimber.

"And I'm going."

"You are not. You're my ..."

"Your what?" Cardi jumped up and squared off with Kimber. "I'm not your mate. You never claimed me. I don't think you ever will. I don't think you want to. So, I'm breaking up with you."

"Breaking up with me?" Kimber sounded out each word individually.

"You heard me."

"Hey!" shouted Beryl. "Where is my mate?"

"She's in Leander's room," said Ari.

Ari leaned against a wall. He was wearing his white karate uniform with the belt loosely tied at his waist. His grin was that of the Cobra Kai sensei in that *Karate Kid* movie when he challenged the untried Daniel to a fight with his champion.

"But you'll probably want to knock first."

Everything went green. Beryl put his feet into motion, leaving behind the shouting match happening between Cardi and Kimber about the status of their relationship.

Beryl followed Poppy's scent down the hall. He knew where Leander's room was, having come to this den many times in his youth. After that fight a few days ago, he doubted he'd be invited here again.

But here he was. In the belly of the lions' den. His claws out and fire scratching to get out of his throat.

He knew he couldn't go into Leander's room, flames blazing. Poppy was in there. Beryl also knew that, unlike Ari, Leander was respectful of others' things.

Except, Beryl had nearly killed the man a few days ago. What if Leander hadn't forgiven him? What if he decided retribution was in order? Beryl's life, namely Poppy, for the life Beryl had nearly taken?

As Beryl stood before Leander's door, locked in uncertainty, he heard voices murmuring behind the door. Those voices didn't sound like signs of duress. They didn't sound like sounds of aggression either.

Beryl reached for the knob and turned. The door didn't budge. He looked down and found there was a bar there. They'd been locked in the room together. From the outside.

"I may be big, but I mean no harm. I have a lot of muscles, but also a lot of charm. There's love in my heart, I really mean it. And my brain is much larger than a peanut."

Beryl stepped back from the door with a wince. Leander was spouting his awful rhymes. The lion had shared his love of poetry with Beryl when they were younger. Beryl had tried not to laugh ... and failed. Leander had been bigger at the time and had put Beryl in a chokehold. The lion made him promise to keep his secret.

"That was ..." Poppy's voice trailed off with what

sounded like uncertainty, but then picked back up, "... very rhyming."

"Thank you." Leander's tone was bright with gratitude. "Did you know Andre the Giant? He played a poet in the film *The Princess Bride*."

"Yes, I've seen that movie."

"Have you met him? What's he like?"

"I haven't met him. He died like twenty years ago."

"He ... what?"

Beryl had heard enough. He lifted the wood blocking the door and pulled it open. Both Poppy and Leander looked up, not in shock. Leander's face morphed from annoyance to worry. Poppy's features went from relaxed to joy and then to wariness.

They were sitting cross-legged on the bed. There was plenty of respectable distance between the two. But still, Beryl's dragon didn't like another unmated male close to his female. The room went emerald green as the dragon took over.

CHAPTER TWENTY-SIX

*D*arkness filled the doorway. But the only thing Poppy saw was the light in his green eyes. She'd once dreaded it every time Bruce darkened her bedroom doorway. Her heart skipped a few beats, and her core warmed at Beryl's presence.

"It's not what it looks like," she said.

His only response was a low grumble. His gaze was riveted past her to Leander. The lion shifter held perfectly still on the mattress, his gaze never leaving Beryl.

Oh, no. They were going to fight. The thing Poppy had come here to prevent was about to happen.

"Beryl," she came to her knees on the bed,

holding her hands up. "I want you to be calm and not Hulk out."

He blinked once. His head turned slowly toward her. The green still overwhelmed his pupils. But he didn't look angry. He didn't look like a beast filled with bloodlust. His green gaze was clear, focused, intelligent.

"I came to try and stop the fight," she said.

"I figured as much."

He reached for her, and she came to him. His hold was tight, smothering, perfect. But the moment she thought she would happily take her last breath and willingly drown in his scent, Beryl let her go. His gaze once again landed on Leander.

Leander was standing. There was a wide berth between him and Beryl. Still, he held up his hands. "This was my mother's idea."

"I figured that out, too," said Beryl. "Poppy came here with my scent on her, and Leona forced the two of you in here somehow."

"Yeah." Leander lowered his hands. "That's exactly what happened.

"Leander doesn't want to fight either. He's a pacifist and a romantic poet."

"We really don't need to advertise that, Pop," said Leander.

A menacing rumble came from Beryl's chest.

Leander winced. "Nicknaming your mate was probably not a good idea."

"That is if she still wants to be my mate." Beryl gulped and looked away.

"You know what?" said Leander. "I'll just get out of your way. But if you're going to do it on my bed, please take the sheets with you."

Poppy rounded on the man she loved. "What are you talking about? Of course, I still want to be your mate."

"I don't know that I can do this, Poppy."

"Do what?"

"Be him." He waved his hands over his large body.

"Be who?"

"Professor Hulk," he said. "I don't always think before I act. I don't always ask before I punch. My instinct is to protect what I love, and more than anything that is you."

Beryl's hands went to his head. He squeezed his eyes shut and kneaded his temples. Poppy brushed his hands away and took over the job for him.

"That's not true. Beryl, I chose you because you fought for me. I chose you because you think about my happiness and my comfort in everything you do."

He opened his eyes. Brown churned inside emerald with licks of fire at the edges of his pupils.

"I chose you because you demand that I treat myself as well as you treat me. I chose you because you made me, a rough speck of dirt, into a treasure."

"You are a treasure." He breathed the words as he kissed each of her fingertips. His breath was shaky as his lips brushed her skin.

"And you're my treasure," she said. "Which is why I'm going to have to punish you."

"Punish me?"

Poppy nodded. "For disparaging what I hold most dear in the world, you need to learn your lesson."

A slow, wicked smile began at the corner of Beryl's mouth.

"I'm going to lick your treasure spot," she said, fondling the front of his pants where she found a ready bulge. "You're going to stand there and take it. If you dare to tell me to stop, I'll lick you for five minutes longer. Do you understand me?"

"Yes, my treasure."

Beryl raked his fingers through her hair. With a

twist of his wrist, he craned Poppy's head back and claimed her with a searing, brutal kiss.

"Did you really doubt me?" Poppy asked when she caught her breath.

"No," he said. "I doubted me. I wanted to deserve you."

"We deserve each other. Now, can we go home? I don't want to do it on Leander's sheets. I want to do it on our sheets."

Beryl unfurled his wings and wrapped her inside them. He carried her out of the lion's den, past an approving Leander, an angry Leona, and a still arguing Kimber and Cardi.

On the way to their bed, he showed her some of the sights of her new world. Poppy paid the wonders little heed. The only thing she was intent on exploring in the near future was the green of her dragon's gaze, the mountain that was his chest, and the valley that was his lips.

Kimber's head ached. It had been a constant ache for the last three years of his life. In human reality, it was three decades as time in the Veil moved differently than in the realm of the Goddess' favored creation. Ever since the highly favored human known as Cardi came to stay, he'd developed a constant pounding right behind his temple.

Every sacrifice Kimber had known had arrived with tears in her eyes. He'd seen slight women arrive with crowns on their heads tremble when the dragons approached. He'd seen stout women in rags dissolve as they saw the size of their captor.

Not Cardi. There had been fire in her gaze and in her spirit. Cardi arrived in flannel pajamas, fuzzy socks, and she'd brought their whole weyr down to their knees.

The slip of a girl faced off against seven dragons and didn't blink, not once. Kimber would be in awe of her if his dragon hadn't wrapped its massive body around her painted pinky finger. The tiny human was able to shake down his beast for her every desire. Pretty soon, Kimber came to realize that the female he'd claimed was a manipulative, spoiled child.

But this latest stunt was dangerous. What had she been thinking of walking into a lion's den? Izem had been hovering over her, preparing to pounce, to devour her. But now the cub was in Kimber's grasp. His dragon barred his teeth, ready to tear the furball's throat out.

"Kimmy! Kimmy, let him go."

The man in Kimber wanted to taste blood. But his dragon, ever wrapped around Cardi's thumb, came to heel at her plea. No, not a plea. Her demand. Cardi never pleaded. She always expected to get what she wanted.

"Mine," his beast growled low in Izem's ear.

"Get off of him," Cardi demanded.

"He was going to bite you," growled Kimber.

"He wasn't going to bite me," said Cardi. "He was going to kiss me."

Kimber's mouth fell open along with his hand. Izem dropped to the ground like a stone. Kimber turned his glare on Cardi.

She stood there, defiant as ever. All limbs and big hair. And ridiculous clothes. Her face was painted in bright pinks and purples. Her petulant lip stuck out.

Had he heard her right? "He was going to kiss you?"

"Yes," she lifted her chin. Then doubt curled her brow. She turned. "You were going to kiss me, right?"

The cub raised his head, even though he was still on the floor. "I was."

Kimber's vision iced over. "You were going to kiss my mate."

"She's not your mate," said the cub coming to stand. "You've had her for years and you've never claimed her."

"She's a child."

The cub turned to look at Cardi. His eyes roamed her body appreciatively. His incisors sharpened to fine points. "There's nothing childish about that tight, little body."

Cardi's cheeks turned as red as her hair. She bit

her lower lip with her pearly white tooth. Her lashes lowered and she looked appreciative.

Kimber had never seen such a look on her face before. Then the spell broke. Her eyes flashed up to him and there was the defiant girl he knew.

"Don't you growl at him," she chided. "He's asked me on a date. What do you think of that?"

What did he think of it?

No one could ask her on a date. She belonged to him. Kimber had marked her after winning the challenge against his father. Was this cub challenging him now?

Or... wait.

There was a challenge going on here. Both he and the cub were being manipulated. The dull ache started in the back of Kimber's head. He was not in the mood for one of her games. But he had no choice.

That was the thing about sacrifices. Dragons were completely devoted to them while they lived. None had ever lived as long as Cardi. Because of her long life with the dragons, she'd learned all the loopholes and tricks. It was why he had incessant headaches. He was constantly warring with his inner beast to please her.

Cardi would make some ridiculous demand. His

beast would want to fulfill her desires. The man was the only one who would look at the consequences. It was like Kimber was dealing with two children. One whined from without the other from within.

He knew what both girl and dragon wanted; for him to claim her. To take her to bed and seal their fate. At first, he'd resisted because he knew all too well the fate of a sacrificed woman. He'd never wanted that kind of blood on his hands.

And then he'd learned that Cardi had fire in her blood. She was half-dragon, which meant she'd likely survive the birth of whelps. He'd known that for months now. So what was holding him back?

Well, the fact that she was still a manipulative, spoiled child as evidenced further by this little stunt.

Really? A cub? As if that would get him to throw her down and breach her virgin flesh.

His dragon growled low. His claws broke the pads of his fingers. His incisors dripped.

He didn't miss the gleam in Cardi's eyes. She had him, and she knew it.

"You only marked her," Izem was saying. "And that was years ago, decades in her time. There must be some kind of statute of limitations on dibs."

Dibs? "She's a person," growled Kimber. "Not a toy ball."

"But my boy is right," said Leona.

Kimber's headache increased at the appearance of the lioness.

"If you have no plans to use the object for it's intended purpose, you should return it," said Leona.

"Cardinal is under my protection," said Kimber.

"But is that where she wants to be?" asked Leona.

They all turned to Cardi. The red flush was gone from her cheeks. Her shoulders weren't so straight with certainty. Good. She needed to be concerned. She needed to know what it was like outside his protection.

"I..."

He felt relief at her hesitation. Good, she was coming to her senses. Kimber raised a brow at her. Unfortunately, Cardi never backed down. She was worse than the triplets.

Her shoulders snapped back. Her chin jutted up.

"I don't know if it's where I want to be anymore," she said. "I think I'd like to explore other options."

Kimber knew better. Cardi was still a child. Still prone to tantrums and games. This was nothing more than a game. Another way to get his attention.

Right? It had to be. Right?

Cardi is trying to play Kimber.
But this game is not going to go as she's planned.
She'll learn that a dragon will break all the rules
when he plays for keeps.

Watch this showdown take place in "
The Dragon's Willing Sacrifice
the third book in the Last Dragons Series.

Want to know how the Veil became closed in the
first place?
Read the forbidden romance that started it all when
a Valkyrie fell for a dragon and a human sacrifice
slipped back through the Veil while they were
kissing.

The Valkyrie's Claim
is a free story written for my Reader Group.
If you'd like your copy, just come on over and join us.
http://bit.ly/InesReaders

ALSO BY INES JOHNSON

Lover of fairytales, folklore, and mythology, Ines Johnson spends her days reimagining the stories of old in a modern world. She writes books where damsels cause the distress, princesses wield swords, and moms save the world.

You can sign up for her mailing list and receive alerts and free reads at http://bit.ly/InesReaders.

The Last Dragons

Dragon's Reluctant Sacrifice

Dragon's Ambivalent Sacrifice

Dragon's Willing Sacrifice

www.ingramcontent.com/pod-product-compliance
Lightning Source LLC
Chambersburg PA
CBHW031254160726
47993CB00001B/152